Redemption

Alchemy Series Book Four

Donna Augustine

Line edit by
Devilinthedetailsediting.blogspot.com

Copy edit by Expresseditingsolutions.com

For Cait

Chapter One

Beginning Again...Again

"What do you mean you're leaving?" I asked Cormac, as he stood across the living room of the penthouse with his back to me. "Cormac, answer me. What are you talking about?"

He didn't turn around and his entire frame seemed to tense at my words. I knew he been more on edge these last few days, but who wouldn't have been, considering the situation. This was the first time since I'd known Cormac that I'd ever seen him this out of control.

And for Cormac, this was indeed out of control. Every move he made was deliberate, and now...I didn't know if I could put into words the barely constrained energy pouring off of him.

We'd just walked in when he sent everyone else away. I knew they'd felt it too. I saw it in Dodd's concerned eyes and Dark's uneasy gait. Even Burrom had kept his comments brief on parting.

I'd known whatever he was planning on telling me wasn't going to be good, but this? He couldn't be serious. Cormac was my rock. He was everyone's anchor. The man who would always remain solid, standing there when things got bad. Now he was...leaving? No, he couldn't really mean this.

I watched him turn, and his eyes met mine for just the briefest of moments before moving on. That's when it really hit. My world started to crumble to the ground around me. Cormac couldn't look at me. He was really going to do this.

"Talk to me. What is going on?" If he would just talk to me, I could get control of this. Cormac didn't leave his people. It went against the very grain of who he was.

"I've got to leave."

Maybe he was talking about a day or so. Maybe it was just a scouting mission or something. Even as the thoughts ran through my head, I knew it wasn't the case but I couldn't stop hoping.

"Where do you have to go? Is it a food run?"

"Just...away. It's...I have to leave."

His body finally released from its tense position, but it wasn't an improvement. Cormac's eyes were wild as he started to move about the living room, no real destination apparent.

"What are you talking about? Talk to me, please!" I finally got my legs to unfreeze from the shock of what he was saying, and crossed the room to where he was and gripped his arm. I knew I was crying. I felt the tears running down my cheeks and I didn't care. "We've got almost three thousand more Fae and wolves here. You can't leave now. I can't do this alone." My fingers dug into his arms, a death grip and one I wouldn't relinquish, trying to hold him to me.

"I'm sorry. I thought I had it under control."

"Had what under control? Is it the new wave of magic?"

When the portal opened three days ago, it sent another shock wave of magic rippling through the world. It hadn't affected me, but I'd felt the raw power of it rushing through our existence. Could feel the fingers of it clawing even deeper into everything there was, shredding what little normalcy that had initially been spared. I saw the acceleration of differences in sheer numbers of humans who were changing. It was akin to a steroid shot. The percentage of *changed*, the people who were becoming different because of the exposure to magic in everything around us, hovered at ten percent. Now, it was closer to fifty.

He finally really looked at me. "I don't know what is going to happen if I stay. What I'll do. I can feel it pulling at me, gnawing away at my body, my thoughts, the very core of who I am and I can't seem to stop it. I have to go."

This doesn't have to be that bad. Maybe it won't be that long. "How long? A couple of days? What are you talking about?"

His attention riveted back to me again and I saw such sadness in his blue gaze that I knew it before he spoke.

"I don't know." The despair I heard in his voice

felt like a virus latching onto my soul. "Dodd will help you, if you need him."

"Dodd? He barely leaves his room because of Sabrina." He just needed to understand that he couldn't leave and then he'd stay.

"He'll step up, but you won't need him."

I collapsed at his feet, my whole body wracked with sobs. I really wasn't going to be able to stop him. Desperation so thick, like I'd never felt before even in my darkest days, suffocated me until it was hard to drag air into my lungs.

"Please, Cormac, I can't do this without you." I grabbed his leg in front of me. "Please, I'm begging you. I don't beg and I'm on my knees begging you. I don't want to do this without you." I was gripping onto him for dear life. He couldn't leave me like this. He wouldn't. "I can't do this," I repeated. He didn't understand.

"I'm sorry." His voice was so soft I barely heard it.

And then I was hugging nothing but air. I frantically scanned the room, but he was gone.

I curled up into a ball on the ground where he'd stood seconds ago and I fell apart. What was I going to do? He'd left me. He'd left everyone.

I didn't get up or move, just huddled there. My head was pounding with a headache. I'd never imagined how much I could cry.

I'd thought I'd hit bottom.

But I hadn't. This, right here, right now, this was what the bottom felt like. When you didn't want to even crawl off the floor. The couches were only a few feet away, but I didn't move from the spot where he last stood. The possibility of this happening had never entered my mind, which made the force of the blow that much worse. I'd figuratively shown my vulnerable underbelly and gotten punched in the gut for my mistake. Now I would pay the price.

I'd begged him to stay for everyone, when the truth was, all I'd cared about was my own need of him.

I might have lain there for hours if Dark hadn't started frantically pounding on the door, calling for Cormac.

Dark was the lone wolf, literally, that I trusted. A tall blond with a pretty boy face, he looked more like a skateboarder than a monster in disguise. He'd sided with us against the wolves too many times to count and if he was looking for Cormac, he wouldn't be leaving until he found him. He looked to Cormac with all the adoration due an esteemed older brother.

As the banging continued, I knew I had to get up. If not for the right reasons, one of which could be the desire to stand on my own two feet, then for my pride. I wouldn't let anyone see what he'd done to me, what I'd been reduced to by his leaving.

"I'm coming," I screamed, and I immediately gripped my head, cringing at the pain my own voice caused.

I pulled myself to my feet and wiped the dampness from my cheeks. I was sure my eyes were red and puffy but nothing could be done for that. I pinched my cheeks to get a little quick color before I unlocked the door.

He was so agitated that he didn't even notice my disheveled state as he brushed past me into the penthouse.

"Where's Cormac?" he asked, looking around.

"What's wrong?" I asked, trying to disguise the hoarseness of my voice.

"What's wrong with you?" he asked, and I knew I hadn't disguised it well enough.

I turned quickly so he didn't have a chance to examine me too well.

"You don't look so hot," he continued, I guess having seen enough.

"Nothing. I think I'm getting a cold. I was about to make some tea. Want some?" I asked, finding an excuse to not look directly at him.

"No, thanks. I need to find Cormac. We're supposed to go on an overnight gas scouting trip and one of the new wolves is being a pretentious ass, claiming he's the group leader and trying to dictate when we leave."

Our gas was once again running dangerously

low, like it had so often since The Shattering. The Shattering was the name we'd given the chain of events that had caused our civilized world to cease to exist. It was the line of demarcation. Before it, there had been hospitals and schools, due process and court systems.

Now, on the most generous day, we survived in what could be termed at best, organized chaos.

Fuel sources were a constant problem. We still needed to run the generators for the funny phones hooked up to our own little system, computers and countless other things. Some places in the castle still had modern heating that required electric. But torches, or "old school lamps," as some liked to joke, were becoming more and more common.

"I really need Cormac." Dark drew my attention back to him as he was still searching the penthouse.

"Cormac had to leave for a little while." *He split town and we're all screwed...again.*

That got Dark's attention instantly, as he swung back to stare at me. "What do you mean?"

His eyes darted around as if he still expected to see Cormac walking in. The panic was starting to form, as I'd feared it would. Dark had always looked to him for direction. Everyone did, or used to. Effortlessly, he had always taken the lead, anchored everyone around him. Now we were adrift. This was going to be a painful transition and

I hoped we wouldn't crash into too many icebergs during the journey.

I fussed with the little hotplate hooked up to a portable solar battery that was heating my tea water. I was trying to keep my hands moving, to disguise the shaking, as I thought up something that would calm him.

"With the way the weather is getting so cold and the threat of the senator looming, he thought it would be a good idea to possibly scout out a better locale for us to move to. Somewhere that would be more efficient to heat and is easier to defend." The lies spewed out of me easily, born of desperation.

"He never said anything." Dark turned from me and I surreptitiously watched his brow furrow and the corners of his lips pull inward. He looked down, as if trying to digest the new information that didn't sit well with his palate.

"It had to be done." I shrugged, feigning nonchalance, as if it wasn't the exact opposite of what Cormac would do. "He'll find a safer place for us, with better resources." After destroying the world as we knew it, what were a couple of lies? I was grateful for the fact that I couldn't easily die, because when I went, I was afraid the destination might be a bit warmer than I liked.

Then again, it might not be too bad. I could end up a VP, with my current resume littered with the death and destruction I'd accidentally wrought.

Perhaps I'd get my own fiery suite with a little imp lap dog.

"How long will he be gone?"

I swallowed past the lump in my throat and tried to find my voice. This one was a whopper. "I'm sure it won't be long, but I don't have an exact time frame." Tired of waiting for water to boil, I walked across the room and fiddled with some of the papers Cormac had left on the table. I flipped through with mock deep concern and furrowed my brow in an effort to mimic how Cormac would've acted if he were here. I needed to seem confident and in charge, not scared shitless like I really was.

I looked back up at Dark. "Go on the scouting mission without him. Take Sharon instead. She's extremely capable and always willing to fill in. Tell the new guy I want to see him up here in ten minutes."

A day ago, I would've heard about this problem but it wouldn't have been a concern. Cormac would've handled it. He would have talked with the new guy and that would have been that. He would've fallen in line, the way they always did.

Dark was scowling more deeply, as if trying to find his mental footing with the new chain of command. It took him a second of adjusting before he said, "Okay. I'll send him up." His forehead smoothed over and he started to make small talk that I barely comprehended but nodded and made enough of the right responses to pull off. A few minutes later, I watched him walk out of the apartment, completely comfortable with the bullshit I'd just fed him.

I, in comparison, was shaking as I sank into the chair closest to me and dropped my head onto the table. The absence of noise in the penthouse was deafening. I felt my eyes burning with tears I wouldn't shed. He didn't deserve them. Today, Cormac had crushed me; I wouldn't let his abandonment destroy anyone else.

Three Months Later

I felt a quick tremor shoot through the castle as I walked down the stone hallway, a small echo of the ones that had contributed to the destruction of our world. They had been much stronger again, right after the portal had opened last time. The earthquakes hadn't simply stopped after that night, but lingered on. Every so often, when you least expected it, the earth shook and reminded everyone of our feeble position on this planet. For me, it was also a constant reminder of my mistakes.

In addition, the last opening flooded The Lacard with nearly three thousand Fae and wolf refugees; men, women and children. When the new arrivals spilled in, in desperate need and deserving of compassion, all I could think of was that they were more mouths to feed.

I'd written anyone left on Vitor's planet off as dead, or as good as, since I'd never thought to see them again. It was amazing they'd even managed to get a portal open. I still didn't know how they'd pulled it off. After questioning them, it seemed they weren't quite sure either.

The responsibility for allowing them to stay here weighed heavily upon my shoulders, but I hadn't been able to push them out into the world as it was now. It didn't matter. We'd survive. If I've learned anything lately, it's that desire can and will sometimes defeat even the worst odds. "Can't" was no longer a word in my vocabulary, though the words "Can" and "Yes" weren't exactly up there in use, either. "Have" *to* seemed to be the hot word of the moment.

But the hardest thing about remembering that day was the reminder of Cormac's abandonment, less than seventy-two hours later. Months had now passed without a word. He could be dead. It might have been easier if he were. That thought used to bring me to my knees, but not anymore. He'd left and I wouldn't shed another tear for him. I wouldn't romanticize what could've been. In the end, he'd shown his true colors. I refused to rationalize those actions into something forgivable.

I took a right turn down another hallway. I'd crammed our new refugees into every last available space. This part of the casino had gone full on castle, one completely devoid of electricity.

On the surface, The Lacard and its inhabitants had been left seemingly unmarred, but the damage was there; you just couldn't see this kind of destruction on the surface. Now, as things calmed down and one by one people succumbed to sleep, the effect of this horrible reminder showed its true form.

At this time of night, the only thing I should have heard was the burning of the torches, the sounds of my solitary footsteps and the soft breaths of slumber. Instead, the near silence was disturbed with the sound of people rousing in the grip of night terrors. The screams of people waking in fear would be this generation's version of bad elevator music.

I should be asleep as well, but when I stayed still my doubts surfaced and memories I wished I could abolish ran through my brain, taunting me, slamming into me with regrets. I paced the halls until I could barely stand and I didn't have another ounce of strength. Until I knew for sure it was safe. When I was positive with absolute surety that the moment I lay upon the bed I had so briefly shared with Cormac, exhaustion would immediately claim me. Then, I too would rise sometime in the night, a cold sweat on my skin and screams torn from me against my will.

So, I walked the halls night after night, among friends and others who I knew were my enemies. They were here, the ones that had killed my mother. I didn't have a shred of proof. Only a small percentage of wolves had survived; just as our world had been ravaged, so had theirs. It appeared our worlds had been more connected than we'd ever realized. The storms that hurt our world had wiped out their entire planet. There was nothing left for them. They'd come through the portal, starving and bedraggled, with nothing but the few possessions they carried.

But I knew in their midst, the murderers had survived. Just as I knew someone was watching me right now, even though I couldn't see them. It wasn't logical but neither was anything else, anymore. Mortals were morphing into mystical creatures from fairy tales almost daily. Thinking logically about what might come was a waste of time.

When I heard footsteps rushing toward me, I swung around quickly, prepared to fight, but stopped short at the familiar face.

"How long have you been following me?" I asked Dodd.

"I've been looking for you for an hour."

Dodd hadn't been my secret stalker. I trusted him almost as much as I had once trusted Cormac. There might be a warning in there somewhere, but I refused to consider it. Other than being a reformed rake, he fell solidly into the good guy list. Hell, even the women he'd dated, and I use the word *dated* loosely, still liked him.

I looked over his shoulder, trying to catch sight of what had sent a tingle down my spine earlier. There was no one to be found and the feeling was gone. Whoever had been watching me was gone.

"Here," Dodd said as he handed me a sheet of paper with the torn edges.

Send Jo out. Or else!

It was written in red crayon, complete with horrible penmanship.

"Pretty funny," I said, handing the sheet back to him.

"Yeah, but I don't think it's a joke. There are lightning bugs flying back and forth in front of the door."

I'd figured as much. I wondered how many bugs it had taken to hold the crayon. They were resourceful little creatures. After The Shattering, lots of things I'd never thought possible had happened. One of the byproducts was a small group of lightning bugs that could speak. But even though they could, they seemed to be quite selective in who they chose to communicate with.

"Did you talk to them?" I didn't know why I

bothered asking the question. He wasn't even *changed*. That was another thing I'd confirmed in the last few months. Birds of a feather *do* tend to flock together. *Changed* were drawn to others like them and to me. I wasn't *changed,* but I was linked just as deeply to the same magic they were and I guess that sufficed.

"I tried," he said, confirming that the rumor mill, even in the worst of times, still cranked full speed ahead. I'd never discussed the bugs with him directly.

He tucked his hands into the pockets of his sweat suit. "They fly away every time someone gets close." He shook his head, perhaps a touch disappointed. I didn't blame him. Talking to bugs wouldn't ever be a super power claim to fame but it did have a novelty appeal.

"I'm going to go see what they need," I said as we headed toward the staircase together. "How's Sabrina?" I hadn't seen her since we'd returned. I thought to the night we'd gotten back from the senator's territory, when it seemed that things were turning the corner. She had sat next to Dodd on the couch, leaning into him for support, looking like a broken doll. But even as battered as she'd been, I thought she was going to be okay. I wasn't anywhere near as certain anymore.

"She's...I don't know. But she'll be fine." His voice was firm on the last sentence, as if he could will her mind to heal by his sheer determination.

"She will be. She's strong." I let it drop, hoping I was right.

"Should I come with you?" Dodd asked.

I knew he would, even though he was vulnerable to the rippers, the man-eating monsters and the stuff of nightmares, who lingered close by at night. I shook my head. "Thanks, but they'll just freeze up if I have company."

I waved him off and I was relieved to part. I didn't have enough lies left to keep talking and I knew the Cormac questions would be coming soon. *Where is he? Is he coming back soon? Did he say he'd send word?* They always did.

I entered the stone lobby that looked so much different to when I'd first come here. It was all massive stone. Large wooden doors replaced the glass modern ones and I could feel the draft coming from them before I got within ten feet.

I waved off the two Keepers standing guard. No one questioned my right to do anything anymore, one of the few perks to being in charge. Too bad it wasn't enough to offset the mind numbing stress of responsibility. I didn't see faces anymore; I saw mouths to feed and bodies to clothe.

As soon as I stepped outside, the frigid air blasted my skin, my breath visible in the night. I wrapped my arms around myself, rubbing the skin left exposed by a t-shirt that would have been perfectly adequate six months ago. I should've stopped for a jacket but I hadn't wanted to leave the lightning bugs waiting any longer.

The same evening the wormhole had opened, an even colder arctic chill fell onto the city. I was never one for conspiracy theories, but sometimes you've got to embrace a coincidence for what it is. I just hoped it didn't last too long or spread too far. If this was the weather pattern in California, all the farms' produce we hadn't tapped into yet would be spoiled before we got there. Silly things we'd taken for granted before were life and death now. Who'd have thought, a year ago, that starvation might be what wiped out mankind?

It didn't take more than a few minutes for the lightning bugs to swarm over. I knew they were my bugs when one showed off her blinking pink tail instead of the standard yellow.

"Hi, Jo," a little chorus of voices sang out.

"Look, Jo." Pinky, as I now thought of her, was flashing her tail purple.

"You're such a show off," Charlie said. He was the one whose tail was a hair dimmer than the rest.

"You're just mad because you're dull," Pinky shot back. "You can't even do yellow well."

She did have a valid point. She flew around him, flashing an alternating pink and purple light. If I could make out her features, I was sure I'd see a smug face that matched the tone.

"You take that back!"

"What did I tell you guys about fighting?" I used to try to stay out of their bickering. Then, one night, things went bad. Fred was still flying crooked due to his bent wing. I wanted to ask how he was doing, but he was very bitter and the reminder alone could make things go south quickly.

"Sorry, Jo." Pinky stopped swirling.

I'd discovered on past visits that there were only a small percentage of lightning bugs that could speak. They called the other bugs dumb. I'd tried to determine if it was the same percentage of bugs as the changed to human ratio, but the bugs couldn't count that high.

"Would you like to come in? It's pretty cold out here." Their flying seemed to be a bit more sluggish than normal. I knew they were bugs. They had probably outlived a normal lightning bug's lifespan already and I couldn't lose another body, not even a little one.

"Oh no! We don't go to the light," Todd explained. I recognized him by the slightly deeper voice. He was the James Earl Jones of the bug world.

"Are you sure? It's safe in there and it's so cold out here." Not to mention the penthouse was awfully lonely at night. Even bickering bugs would be an improvement.

"No, we've lost too many to the light. First rule

of Light Club is you don't go into the light," Pinky said.

"I bet I know the second rule."

"No, Light Club is a secret. You couldn't possibly know."

"Let me give it a try. Second rule of Light Club is don't go into the light?"

Little gasps of shock ran through the swarm.

"I just hope your third doesn't have anything to do with fighting."

"Of course not! We'd never fight, well...not anymore." No one added *since Fred*, but it was silently understood.

"What's the third rule, then?"

No one spoke and I watched them fly into a little cluster and whisper so low that it would be impossible for any human to hear.

Finally, Pinky spoke. "It used to be that your first night in Light Club, you had to go into the light."

I sucked a breath in through my teeth, knowing where this was going.

"After Chuck, we don't do that rule anymore."

"Chuck?"

"It was horrible. He went too far. He was like that, a risk taker to the end. All we heard was a horrible zapping noise. He managed to escape but he only made it to the window landing before he collapsed, exhausted. We screamed and screamed but he just didn't have the energy left. His last words were 'better to die young than to fade away'. It was the last time we saw him."

I heard the footsteps crunching in the snow, coming from the direction of the castle, and knew the lightning bugs weren't going to be happy.

And right on cue, they chimed in. "He's coming again. Got to go!"

I looked behind me to see Burrom approaching. "I thought you liked Burrom?"

"Nope. He's off the VIB list!"

"You mean VIP?"

"No, VIB. Very Important to Bugs."

"Why'd he get bumped?"

"We heard him say we were 'just bugs.' Yeah, well he's just stupid."

The bugs flew off, making little giggling noises, and I shivered as I turned around and watched Burrom approach. It was as if the Earth and night conspired for him. The moon hung full in the sky and glistening snowflakes started to fall as he walked the distance to me. The light from castle silhouetted his form, leaving just a hint of detail. And if I squinted my eyes just so, I could almost pretend it was Cormac.

But it wasn't. Cormac was gone. He'd walked out the door and I'd closed it. So I didn't squint and I didn't pretend. I accepted it for what it was and I used the pain to build the armor around my heart for the day he might return.

Burrom pulled off the jacket he had on and laid it upon my shoulders and followed up the gesture by pulling it closed in front of me. It was such a boyfriend act, but I didn't think he realized it, and I let it go unspoken. He had a carousel of women coming and going so often I think it was becoming second nature to him to behave like that.

"What's going on?" He looked in the direction of where the bugs had flown off.

"Nothing." I pulled the jacket snug to me and felt his leftover warmth. I turned and lifted my face to the snow. It was coming down heavily now and presented a clean and stark contrast to the destruction it was softly coating.

"Come on." I turned and walked closer to the drawbridge. It had once been a piece of metal that had lain over the cracks in the surface, created by the first of the great storms. The magic saw fit to turn it into antiqued wood with old iron fittings. It even supplied a mechanism for raising and lowering it over the rushing water below.

Our footsteps echoed loudly as we stepped across and into the middle of what used to be the Vegas strip. The buildings were charred skeletons of what they once were, destroyed and hollowed out. In twenty or thirty years, as a new generation was born and raised, they would never know the brilliance that had once existed where I now stood.

When I closed my eyes on the new landscape, I could still remember the vivid lights.

One day, the picture would dull in my mind's eye, as it would for everyone. Fewer and fewer people would be around to tell the story of the incredible world we had once built. But, with the snow falling and reflecting the silver light of the moon, the world was almost pretty again. Hauntingly beautiful, one might say.

The quiet peacefulness was eerily foreboding. The rippers, strange scaled monsters more fitting for a horror flick that terrorized us on a daily basis, were oddly absent. Burrom and I were the only ones outside.

"It is beautiful." Burrom's voice was deep with a rough timbre.

His face was raised to the sky, seemingly breathing in the environment. If it had been anyone else, I wouldn't have thought twice of the gesture. But it was Burrom, and so he might have been leaching some sort of energy I couldn't see. He took a couple steps farther and reached out his arms, palms up.

"It's glorious."

I watched him slowly circle around. "What's glorious?"

He let out a deep pleasing sound. "The magic. It's so strong and clean, lately." He tilted his head in my direction and opened his eyes, a smile on his face. "I understand why he left."

"Who?" I purposely played stupid hoping he'd take the hint that the subject of Cormac was not open for discussion.

He lifted an eyebrow and I knew he wasn't going to let it rest.

"He was too sensitive to it and kept resisting it." He raised his face again. "Someone who was so intent on control, the way he was, would be unnerved by the flex and flow of it pulsing within him."

He let out a sad sigh of regret as he dropped his arms. "As much as I could stay here all night, I've got to go in. They've been making a real mess of my bar lately."

He walked back toward the castle, now a towering stone structure complete with turrets.

He stopped just long enough to wink at me. "Your secrets are safe with me," he said. "I agree with the lies you've spread." He then continued walking. "It's for the best, until he returns."

I didn't need to ask him why he agreed. It was better for everyone involved that Cormac's disappearance hadn't seemed unplanned and chaotic. People needed reassurances right now, and thinking the one constant figurehead had abandoned them could rock the foundation.

"If he ever does," I yelled after him.

"He will."

Burrom continued into the casino but he'd sounded so positive that hope sparked in my chest and it urged me to chase after him and question what he knew. But that would open up a Pandora's box of emotion I'd sealed away. It wasn't something that I could dip into. If I opened that box, it would break wide.

Chapter Two

A New World Justice

"This is my pack," Rogo said, growling loudly as he faced down his opposition in what was now the great hall. A crowd was forming around them but no one dared to get closer than five feet.

It had been the main casino gambling floor not so long ago, but you would never know it now. There was the same stone as the exterior everywhere you looked, and not the faux stuff, but a foot deep. I knew because I'd had to reopen a few doorways after the magic decided to redecorate. A large walk-in fireplace on one side helped offset the lack of modern heat in the room.

When I'd woken up this morning, I'd discovered we'd lost more electricity sometime in the night while we slept. At least the magic had the decency to supply torches along the walls.

"You aren't wolf enough to man your own pack," the other wolf, Kaz said.

I wasn't surprised the tensions had elevated to this point. Kaz was an alpha wolf who had come through a few months ago. I was more surprised it had taken this long for him to try to assert his dominance. I'd known he was going to be trouble as soon as I saw him standing in the portal, arrogantly demanding entry. His every action had reeked of supremacy.

Rogo surprised me though. I'd figured he would eventually back down and let him take over. Kaz seemed more dominant than Rogo. Guess I was wrong.

Kaz's chest was puffed up and I stood back, debating whether I should intervene. We were supposed to have a meeting in a few hours, to discuss the different contributions. I didn't know wolf politics, but I knew it would be a lot easier to deal with one alpha wolf than a bunch of different fractions like I had to do with Vitor and Burrom.

"We'll see about that," Rogo spat out. "I call Mortem Pugna."

"Accepted," Kaz replied before Rogo had barely finished speaking.

Just great. We were almost out of coffee, I might have to read my daily notes by torchlight, and now these two morons were going to fight to the death before I'd had my quota of caffeine. No wonder this world was so uncivilized. Didn't anyone have manners, anymore? No blood until after I had my coffee. How many times did you have to tell them?

I guess it was time to get involved, sort of. "You'll take it outside," I said as I stepped forward out of the shadows, my favorite place these days. No one could ask you questions you couldn't answer if they didn't see you.

"Don't give me those looks, you have no idea how hard it is to get blood out of stone floors. And don't even tell me the winner will clean it, because you know it will be my issue. Just like Colleen's dog, who's shitting all over the place." It was bad enough the floors were stone, but must they be filthy, too? Couldn't a girl expect some sort of standards in her living conditions, even during the end of the world?

They stood, chests puffed up and still not budging.

"You both know I could take you down. Even paired up it's not looking good for you, so I suggest you heed my warning and take it outside." I pointed toward the doors, like they might have somehow forgotten the direction outside was.

They both growled and I stepped in between them. Just like in a dogfight, it's not normally a good idea to step in between a wolf fight either. I needed to take drastic measures. I was not dealing with another bloodstain.

I put a hand on either chest and pushed. "Not. Here."

They both finally nodded their acceptance. "Outside. Ten minutes," Rogo said.

The wolves disappeared, probably to change form. They usually fought in wolf form. I'd already witnessed a few skirmishes as the wolves integrated into their new positions and places in the pack.

The crowd in the hall around me was on fire, buzzing about what had just happened as Burrom headed over.

"You have to lay off the mother angle. Makes you sound soft." I eyed up his current outfit. Too snug pants and a skin-tight tee.

"That's only because you're naïve. What do you know of mothers? Didn't a maple tree shit you out?"

It was hard to hear his snort over the din of the crowd gossiping. "I take it back. You sound just as you should."

I laughed. I knew how crude that had sounded.

"You're cool with this?" he asked, knowing how I hated the constant fighting.

"I would've stopped it if I wasn't. Besides the needless death aspect, I'm not sure it's worth trying to stop. This one is unavoidable." I couldn't imagine either Kaz or Rogo playing second fiddle for long.

"Do you have a dog in this fight? Pun intended." He stood, feet shoulder breadth apart, arms crossed as if he were discussing a football game that was about to start.

"I'm not fond of Rogo, but he's predictable, if not always controllable. I would prefer him to be the victor, but it will be easier on me either way. One less wolf to negotiate with." I shrugged and leaned against the now empty breakfast service table. "It's efficient, if not pleasant. What I don't get is, what's so wrong about just beating each other to a pulp and calling it a day, like normal people?"

Burrom leaned down closer to me. "It doesn't work for the wolves. If they didn't have the fear of death hanging over the confrontation, there would be constant fighting for alpha."

I pushed up and started heading outside before all the good spots were taken.

"You want to watch?" he asked as he fell into step beside me.

"'Want' isn't the right word. I need to make sure it doesn't get out of hand and others don't try to jump in. Plus, I like to see them action." With the wolves making up about a third of the castle occupants, it was beneficial to have as much knowledge as possible. There was also the other issue of my mother's murderers, which I'd eventually have to deal with.

The crowd forced us to slow as we approached the doors outside. The entire casino was pouring out into the front courtyard to make sure they got a good view of the fight to come. That's my peeps for you, just a good old bloodthirsty horde in every shape and size, furry, winged, scaled, and those were the ones I felt good about. It was the ones with hidden skills and talents that were most likely to take a person out. After all, it's always what you don't see coming that gets you in the end.

"Come on," he said. "You're going to miss your

homework assignment."

We made our way out to the front courtyard, still covered in snow. The air was brisk and chilly. It must have dropped ten degrees since last night.

The crowd parted for me and Burrom, and opened up a spot in front so we'd have a great view of the violence. I eyed him, knowing he'd done something magical to encourage it. He smirked in response.

Everyone was out here, and the ones that weren't hung out any window that was still big enough to allow it. The castle had shrunk so many of them down they were a firefighter's nightmare.

I looked around and felt almost like I were in high school, with all the cliques. Everybody was commingled but separate. The Fae, humans, wolves, Keepers and *changed* were all in their own little clusters.

The crowd parted again as both wolves, Rogo and Kaz, walked out into the center of the circle, both in wolf form. They didn't stand still long but started to circle each other, looking for weaknesses. Rogo was slightly taller and looked like he would have the longer reach. Kaz was wider, probably outweighing Rogo by a good thirty pounds.

The scene was brutal, vicious and barbaric. And it fit our new world like a custom made suit.

Dark stepped up behind us, getting a clear view over my shoulder. He was a wolf too, but everyone knew his allegiance was with the Keepers. He'd been excommunicated from his own kind when he'd decided to join us. If it bothered him still, he didn't show it.

Burrom nodded to him in greeting.

"Hey," I said in a hushed tone, not sure why I was whispering. This was a fight to the death, not an afternoon at the library. Before I could say anything else, Rogo made his move and drew our full attention back to the two combatants.

It was a long swipe that caught Kaz across the ribs. He let out a growl just as a loud cheer rose from the part of the crowd rooting for Rogo. Neither wolf wore anything but their fur, and the crowd could see the fresh gash ripped open, the jagged flesh partially hanging. Blood dripped from the gaping wound, matting in Kaz's fur. It didn't look lethal, just brutally painful. Yeah, I was getting good at judging wounds. After all, this wasn't my first death match.

I was glad Rogo was off to a strong start, but I didn't cheer. I wouldn't show my preference openly; I'd have to deal with whoever won. I'd never cared about politics before The Shattering. I'd blissfully gone through life completely ignorant of elections. Never voted or cared, until the senator. Apparently, living knee deep in the political considerations of every freak known to man was to be my penance for youthful irresponsibility.

I looked at Burrom and saw he was keeping a neutral expression as well, although that wasn't as uncommon for him. Sicko that he was, he actually enjoyed playing politics. I didn't understand how we were even friends.

Rogo got another good blow in that sent Kaz reeling, and he staggered backward. Rogo quickly followed his staggering form, and snapped his jaws, just missing Kaz's neck by less than an inch.

Just as I was becoming confident Rogo might be able to win this one, I saw his stance change slightly. Typical of Rogo, he was getting cocky. That's when I knew it was only a matter of time. He was losing his edge. He thought he had it in the bag. I sighed and refrained from the urge to rip a hand through my hair.

Kaz was already starting to come around again and was beginning to circle. He was sluggish but he was acting more hurt than he really was to lure Rogo in. I could see it in his eyes. They were too sharp in contrast to the way he was moving. You can see pain in a person's face and a werewolf wasn't much different; Kaz was only reading about a three out of ten.

I wanted to smack Rogo and tell him to pay attention, but I couldn't even make eye contact with him. He was too busy prancing around the ring like a popinjay, playing to the crowd. They longed for blood, wanted reparations for their losses and pain, and they weren't particular where they got it. Guilt and responsibility weren't required.

Kaz staggered, falling to his knees, as if struggling from blood loss. Rogo saw the fake opening and eagerly stepped into the trap. I knew what would come next and resisted the urge to turn away. It would've looked weak to the wolves and I couldn't afford any show of vulnerability that could be exploited. I let my vision blur out of focus as Kaz leapt to his feet and took Rogo's head off with a snap of his jaws.

Rogo's body collapsed onto the ground. It bucked and continued to spasm, even as his head rolled a few feet away. Blood pooled bright red on the snow-covered ground beneath him.

The crowd stood hushed, but only briefly, and then erupted into cheers for Kaz. It apparently didn't matter that some of them hadn't been cheering for him in the beginning. They were certainly trying to vigorously make up for it now. Or perhaps they cheered for the newest payment made toward the anger they held. Maybe it was the nearness of death that reaffirmed their own still beating hearts and excited them.

The reason didn't seem to matter to Kaz. He stood in the center, accepting the attention as if it were his due. He turned to where I stood and walked over.

"Meeting. Eight tonight," I said.

Kaz turned away without an acknowledgment. I knew the wolves enough by now to know it was a slight, and so would everyone nearby. Why did the wolves always have to be such a problem? It was a stupid question and I already knew the answer. Their society ran like a pack and an alpha didn't tolerate another alpha's presence. And even though I was twice damned in their eyes, being a female and not a wolf, he considered me an alpha. I guess I could take it as a compliment.

Kaz took about ten steps away and I knew I couldn't let the slight go unanswered. The castle was near to bursting with different races, all scheming for control. In this environment, you couldn't let any cracks show.

I waited, as everyone else watched.

Kaz was about twenty feet away when my voice carried loud enough for everyone there to hear. "Clean up your mess."

Kaz stopped. He stood still and then he waved toward some of his men and pointed to where Rogo's body lay. Then he turned and looked back at me. I was in jeans and a winter jacket that I'd found in an old ski shop, but I felt naked as his eyes went from my toes all the way to my chest and stayed there before finally reaching my face. His large wolf tongue reached out and lasciviously licked his lips, his tongue following the points of his fangs.

I took an aggressive step toward him. "Try it."

He stood his ground as I walked closer to him; not being able to speak in wolf form didn't matter. His puffed up chest said it all. "You sure you want to do this? You might have a lot of backup, but so do I and I guarantee you, I won't go down before I take you out first."

I saw his nostrils flare and his chest rising and falling with his breaths.

I stood an inch from him. He towered over me but I didn't feel scared or intimidated; I had my own blood lust coursing through my veins. I had months of bone crushing disappointment and responsibility, and I was looking for an excuse to unload.

His eyes widened slightly as he stared into my unflinching face and I recognized the expression. I'd been getting it quite often lately.

"No, not crazy, blood thirsty. And know this, I don't care where I get my pound of flesh. I'm just waiting for an excuse." Not a hundred percent true, but close enough that I could pull it off.

He dropped his stare in silent surrender.

"Too bad," I said, and meant it. He turned and walked back to the castle. "Let me know if you change your mind," I called after him in a tone that sounded like I were trying to push a timeshare tour on him, not offering up death on a platter.

Chapter Three

The Bad Man Cometh...

I walked further down the empty Vegas strip, among the towering piles of debris, enjoying several feet of snow and freezing air. Yeah, right. Who was I kidding? I was freezing and I couldn't feel the tip of my nose.

I was stalling. I'd go back soon, but the faces, the questions, the never ending needs and, even worse, the quiet of the penthouse, all waited for me and didn't offer an appetizing evening. I'd return, but not until I had recharged my battery for a minute. I'd stay out here long enough that I could muster up the energy to plaster on the appearance of calmness over my raging emotions.

Before I could stop myself, I wondered if Cormac had felt like this. This could drive anyone to run.

No, I would not give him excuses. I was less prepared for this than he had been and I still stayed. I could've left, but I hadn't. And the staying hadn't been easy, especially not in the beginning. The wolves had been nipping at my position, undermining my control in every way they could.

They still were, but were just being less obvious about it. I knew they'd been picking away at the food supplies in storage. I just didn't know how they were gaining access, yet. I had that area guarded around the clock by Keepers, which meant one of them might be cooperating.

In the beginning, the humans barely tolerated me, until I'd made it clear they could leave if they didn't like the way things were going to be. The Keepers were loyal, but I feared it was simply because they all still expected Cormac to come strolling back any day. Even some of the Fae had tried to undermine me.

I was so lost in my own thoughts it took me longer than it should've to notice the solitary figure approaching. He was about a half a mile away, walking toward me. Squinting my eyes as he approached, I saw long blond locks caught up in the wind as a full-length fur coat flapped around his calves.

My spine stiffened as my brain recognized who it was. He hadn't alerted me that he'd intended to visit, but he rarely did. I tried to tune my senses in to my surroundings but I was pretty sure he'd come alone, like always.

"Josephine." He stopped about twenty-five feet shy of me.

"Senator."

Neither of us spoke as we took each other's measure.

His feminine grey fox coat might have inspired

laughter from someone more naïve, but I'd had enough experience with him to not be lulled in by his flamboyant dress. There was nothing soft about this…man?

I could see from his expression, he found my black cargo pants and hiking boots lacking.

My palms were moist and my pulse raced. I schooled my features into a blank canvas as I stood there, waiting for him to speak. Every time he showed, I expected the worst. Even now, after months of periodic visits with no ill effect.

"Care to take a stroll?" he asked.

"Sure." I shrugged and stepped forward, acting much less agitatedly than I felt. If I could get him to leave peacefully, I'd take the stroll, no matter how distasteful I found his presence. The first visit had been the most disconcerting.

I walked the distance to him and kept walking. He fell into step beside me as we strolled down the strip together.

"Still no Cormac?" He asked a question he already knew the answer to. I didn't know if he was looking for a reaction or trying to rub in the betrayal.

I knew he had spies in the casino. After Cormac left, I hadn't bothered wasting resources and energy on finding out who they were. Sometimes information leaking wasn't such a bad thing, and yes, maybe we didn't have a steady supply of food and resources, but we weren't sitting ducks either, with our increased numbers, and I wanted him to know. I'd also been juggling so many different issues since that I hadn't cared.

I didn't bother responding to his question in a petty attempt to thwart whatever it was he looked to gain.

"I have to say, in spite of myself, I feel impressed. Knowing your mother, I never thought you would be capable of taking charge of that many people."

"I'm not sure if I should be insulted or say thanks." I was surprised at his mention of her. We'd both avoided the topic in the past. These conversations always felt surreal, and not in a good way. I just wanted him to get to the point, sooner rather than later.

"If you had known your mother, you would understand. She was a feckless creature." He flipped a long blond lock away from his face.

He spoke as if I wouldn't have a reason to be annoyed by him discussing her like this. A year ago, I probably wouldn't have been. These days, I had a lot more compassion and understanding for the choices people made. The big ones weren't usually easy. So it galled me but I held my tongue and refrained from getting into a tit for tat insult session.

"Are you here for a reason or did you just feel like strolling in the snow with me?" I asked, hoping to speed things up a bit. I wasn't sure how long he'd been alive, but he had the nonchalance of someone who hadn't watched a clock for decades. I was only newly immortal and a bit more time sensitive.

"We've reached an impasse of sorts and I thought a clearing of the air was in order." He spoke like a scholar and oozed arrogance.

I remembered the first time he'd shown up, just a few weeks after Cormac had left. I'd been petrified of what he'd wanted. We'd spoken a few meaningless words that I couldn't even remember, now. He'd left and I'd collapsed in relief, not telling anyone of his appearance.

A week later, he'd shown up again. I still wasn't clear on why, but he never made any demands or threats. We'd fallen into an awkward pattern of occasional visits. Him showing up and me agreeing to go along with it. I did it to keep myself apprised of the current level of aggression and I started to imagine he was doing it for the same purpose. I viewed it as an awkward truce of sorts, sort of like two divorcées living in different wings of a house and playing polite so the other didn't torch the lawn.

But in all this time, we'd never "cleared the air" and I wasn't sure how much clearing he was looking to do.

"Was there anything in particular you wanted to share?"

"It's not in my best interest to kill you.

Likewise, killing me might have some of the same inherent risks."

He tilted his head toward me with his last words, still acting nonchalantly, as if there were nothing amiss about discussing our mutual destruction.

But, more importantly, he confirmed what Burrom had thought. Whether it was true or not, there were now two different voices expressing a concern over possible repercussions if I were to be killed. I didn't tell him I'd wondered if his death might have the same negative ramifications.

"What did you have in mind?"

"I think that we can mutually exist - perhaps even be of use to each other, from time to time."

I stepped back quickly when he reached into his jacket.

He stopped moving instantly. "I just wanted to offer you a gift of peace, is all." He stood paused, not out of fear but consideration to my alarm.

At my nod, he continued to reach within his pocket. As his hand withdrew, I saw a long red velvet case. He held it out to me and my curiosity got the best of me. I reached forward and took it.

Prying it open, I was stunned by the ruby bracelet lying on velvet.

"This is a peace gift?" I looked back up at him.

"Fit for a queen," he said. "Thirty carats set in platinum."

"I got the distinct impression, on several occasions, that you found me beneath you." Yes, I had a chip on my shoulder. Actually, make that present tense. I *have* a chip on my shoulder. Dealing with him in the past had grown it to an unhealthy size. I'd managed to shrink it down, small enough that it wasn't screaming attitude. But this, after the way he'd treated me in the past - the scorn with which he dealt with me, I couldn't quite rise above. Sometimes it's more fun to roll around in the mud than rise above.

"Like I said, I might have underestimated you." I watched his eyes rove over me again. "You know, you could be quite attractive, if you did something with those clothes."

"Is there anything else?" I tucked the bracelet in my pocket, wondering when I'd ever have an occasion to wear it. A truckload of gas might have warmed me up to him more.

"No, I think that about sums it up."

"Fine. I'm agreed. There will be no aggression from my side. But, from now on, if you want to discuss anything, you will give me three days' notice, delivered by a single human, that you are entering my territory. I will, of course, offer this person safe return."

"And you will do the same?"

"Yes."

He stopped walking, as did I.

"I find these terms acceptable."

"I'm so glad." I said it was such an exaggerated graciousness I was sure he'd realize the insult, but instead he smiled, oblivious.

"I'd offer you my hand but I doubt you'd take it. As I said, you seem a bit savvier than your mother ever was." He tilted his head to the side and squinted his eyes. "I'm surprised with your human emotions you haven't taken one of these opportunities to question me about her."

His eyes were deep and penetrating, as if he could discover my secrets by simply staring. I was fairly certain that wasn't one of his abilities, especially since he missed my mockery. If he had an idea of what I really wanted to do to him, I doubted he'd be offering me gifts.

I wouldn't explain that a part of me was bursting with curiosity. I refused to give him any satisfaction. I shrugged, smiled and turned my back on him, as if I had nothing to fear.

"I'll assume you can find your own way home," I yelled as I left him standing there.

"I anticipate this to be a long and interesting relationship, Josephine," he hollered back and let out a deep throaty laugh that filled the air.

***

It had taken supreme control to keep from

shivering while I was with the senator but I'd managed. Walking into the penthouse, I felt like it was going to take forever to thaw out. As the magic changed the casino, it at least had pity enough to supply fireplaces in the rooms that had been robbed of heat. The penthouse was one of the last areas to lose modern heating but it finally lost the battle, the vents covered by stone one chilly afternoon. At least we could still find wood for fires.

Dark and Dodd were already sitting on the couches in the living room when I arrived. I think being in the penthouse made them feel closer to Cormac, somehow, and I liked the company. I still hadn't told either of them the truth but kept the lie going that Cormac was to return.

As I warmed my hands near the raging fire, I filled them in on the most recent visit from the senator. After he started to come regularly, I'd felt it was best that they knew. If I disappeared one day, I didn't want them to think I'd abandoned them.

"What's that?" Dark asked, looking at the back of my pants where I'd forgotten I'd shoved the bracelet case. I dug it out and tossed it to him. "Token from the senator."

He lifted it out of its velvet and dangled it in the air.

"Whoa, those are high quality," Dodd said. Even with just the light from the fireplace the warm glow of the rubies showed the silk of the large stones. "I knew it."

"You knew what?"

"That's it, I get your next fresh fruit ration," he said to Dark.

"Knew what?" I repeated.

Dodd sat smugly while Dark explained. "Dodd bet me the senator had a thing for you."

"No, he doesn't." I hoped.

"Oh, yes, he does. I, of all people, know what a man after some tail is like," Dodd said, laughing boisterously now. "He's not stopping by to just chat with you this often if he doesn't want in."

I ignored that he was laughing at my expense. It was the first time I'd heard him laugh at anything in months and it lightened my mood.

That was until they started their Cormac game.

"If Cormac was here, he'd kick his ass," Dark said, more to Dodd than me.

"He wouldn't have to. He's so badass the senator probably wouldn't come visit her at all," Dodd replied.

I kept my face toward the fireplace as they continued the, *if Cormac was here* game. I'd been listening to it for months and it seemed to get worse with each passing day. Cormac's pedestal was getting higher, and the taller it got, the thinner my patience ran.

I turned and headed toward my room, to escape from the game, not wanting to hear any more about how the almighty Cormac would've handled it when I wanted to spew the ugly truth that he'd abandoned them. He was probably lying on a beach somewhere warm, having the time of his life.

I knew I was getting a bit carried away in my delusions, but it had been three months. He was either dead, the thought still feeling like a fist around my heart, or doing something he deemed more important than all of us. Either way, I wasn't optimistic.

I'd almost made it out. And in five minutes from now, I was going to have wished I'd left the room just a few seconds earlier and avoided what was about to come next.

"Jo! When do you think he'll be back?" Dark asked.

I sighed and turned back to them. Maybe I should just tell them now. I couldn't keep this lie going forever. They'd eventually succumb to the suspicions as the time grew longer and longer. I was getting more and more questions about when. Why was it taking so long? Even if I could manage to stop myself from counting the days, someone would remind me of how long he'd been gone.

But I saw their hopeful faces and I lied. "I'm sure he's doing everything he can to find a suitable place." A suitable place on the beach with a cocktail and a hot little chickie serving it to him. I turned to leave again but Dodd stopped me.

"I bet you're sorry that you guys didn't get together sooner, huh? All that wasted time while you were figuring things out and then he had to leave."

I felt it coming, the sanity and calmness I kept locked tight around my natural instincts started to strain and crumble under the pressure. And I snapped. I couldn't do it anymore. I couldn't keep up this charade and protect him with my lies.

I walked back into the room and stood in front of the couch where they sat. I decided to get it out as quickly as I could.

"He didn't leave to find a new place for us. He just left." Their jaws dropped. They'd been deifying him and Cormac didn't deserve that. He'd abandoned them, just like he had me. "He never went to find a better place. I lied. I made it up to keep everyone calm."

"I don't understand," Dodd said.

The logic I'd told myself a minute ago had seemed so sound until I watched their faces go from shock to devastation. I still longed for the escape my room offered but instead, I collapsed on the sofa opposite them, not able to abandon them now that I'd ripped the blinders off.

"He was having issues with the magic changing him and he left," I tried to explain and lessen the harm I'd done. It softened it just as much as it had for me. Pulling the knife out didn't undo the stab wound. I looked at their horrified expressions and wished I'd kept my secret.

"He left us?" Dark asked in a soft, child-like voice.

"Yes, I'm sorry." Their faces betrayed their feelings. They were crushed, and I wished I could rewind time and rip out my own tongue. I hadn't done them a favor giving them the truth. I'd been selfish. I had so much anger toward Cormac it was blinding me and corrupting my choices.

"He didn't say he wouldn't come back." I'd thought of his words that day over and over again.

"What did he say?" Dodd asked.

"That he needed to get away." I looked down at the floor as I answered, having a hard time seeing the hurt in their eyes.

"Did he say anything else?" Dark asked.

I shook my head. "I don't think we should tell anyone else about this, okay?" Telling them was bad enough. I couldn't imagine a castle full of these forlorn faces.

Dark nodded and I heard Dodd utter a soft "Yeah," under his breath.

Dodd stood, muttered something about having to check in on Sabrina and left. Dark just sat on the couch.

"Are you okay?" I asked.

"I left my people, in part because I believed in him, in his loyalty."

He hung his head, shoulders drooping. I mentally berated myself again for telling him.

"He loved you, you know that."

"Not enough to stay." He shook his head, now the one avoiding my stare.

It was hard to defend Cormac against the exact same betrayals I felt myself. But I would do it for Dark.

"He wouldn't have left if he hadn't felt like he had to. You know him; he's loyal to the bone. He wouldn't have made this decision unless he felt he didn't have a choice." I spoke the words and I wished I could believe it myself.

"Really? You think so?" His eyes darted up to me, a glimmer of hope.

"Yes." I forced the lie out and didn't look away.

"You think he'll come back?"

"I know he will." I stood, and stretched my legs, hoping I was right, if only for his sake. "Hey, why don't you crash in the extra room? I know you guys are tight in Dodd's suite."

"You sure?"

"Positive. The company would be nice." I walked into my room, Cormac's old room, and shut the door, promising myself that was the last time I'd tell the truth. This honesty crap was for the dogs. I never should have tossed out my *lie about Cormac to all and sunder* policy. I'd learned the hard way. From now on it would be lie, lie and lie some more, if it had anything to do with him. Let them figure it out on their own when he never came back.

Chapter Four

Top Dog

Dinner in the great hall was an odd affair. I didn't normally dine there; too many eyeballs trained on me made it hard to chew. But with all the new residents, and one in particular that liked to play power games, I was trying to keep my ears open. I also wanted to see how the wolves would fall in line, or not, with Kaz as the official alpha.

There was also the spy issue I needed to ferret out. At some point, it wouldn't work in my favor.

I feigned a great interest in my plate of warm canned peas, tuna and instant potatoes. It wasn't a pairing I'd give much praise but, it beat out the spam and applesauce duo of last night. The brownies, thanks to a recent soar in egg production that I still couldn't quite figure out, had saved that meal from becoming a complete loss.

I found an unoccupied shadowy nook and tucked myself in. It was still early in the evening, but even during the day it was getting darker and darker in here, with no electricity. The fireplace was piled with logs to bursting, the tops of the flames so tall they disappeared into the chimney. In normal times, you might have said the heat was on full blast.

As I settled farther into my shadowed corner, I waited as the few people watching me slowly forgot my presence and went back to their idle chatting and dining.

I scanned the entire room, taking in as much detail as I could. The very first thing that struck me was that we lived together and struggled as one, but were more divided than ever.

Fae sat with Fae, humans with humans, and Keepers with Keepers. *Changed*, whose numbers were growing almost daily now, sat in their own spot. The wolves...well, nothing new there. No one ever really mingled with them. They were the big smelly bullies on the playground who the other kids avoided.

I waited, hoping the divide wasn't as bad as it appeared. I watched, looking for any interaction, but nothing. What kind of life would we build if we couldn't even speak with each other? Would we have anything left to rebuild if we couldn't get along, or would we be picked off by the senator, one weak link at a time? Or maybe we'd start picking each other off. I couldn't place blame when I was no better, guilty myself of wanting to shed some blood.

Once again, I wondered at the person I'd become. I was as bloodthirsty as the wolves these days, with maybe even more suppressed rage. Keeping our numbers healthy was the only thing that kept me from exacting my own revenge. That and the fact I didn't have the names of my mother's murderers.

Losing my appetite, I stepped out of the shadows and handed my plate to a *changed* passing by, who willingly took it and thanked me. You didn't leave uneaten food on your plate, and offering a share of your meal was actually considered a gift. I waved off the thanks and left.

I took the stairs two at a time as I headed up to the conference room where we were having our meeting. I paused at Dodd's floor; I desperately wanted to see Sabrina but I wouldn't push. She hadn't left Dodd's rooms since the night we'd gotten back and word had it that even Colleen and Dark, who were in the same suite, didn't see her.

I'd feel out Dodd tomorrow on whether Sabrina was up to visitors yet. I got it, she'd been through an ordeal; but at some point, regardless of what happened, she'd have to join the living again.

I walked out onto the stone floor where the conference room was located. Like almost everything else in this place, it had morphed into some sort of medieval strong hold. I pushed the solid wood of the door open and the full volume of the room hit me as everyone bickered amongst themselves.

Kaz was already there. I guess he decided not to push me any further by coming late, or worse, pulling a no show. Vitor leaned against a wall and was looking better than he had in months, probably due to his sister being here, one of the many refugees who had survived. Burrom was half sitting on the side table and looking, God forgive me for saying this, pretty damn hot. The idea made my skin crawl a bit. I never thought I'd ever view Burrom as attractive. It just felt wrong. Adam was there as the humans' main spokesperson. And Colleen. A little tingle of pride made me smile that Colleen was there as the *changed* representative.

And then there was me, currently in charge of this chaotic and quite often disobedient group. I stepped over to the head of the table and leaned a hip on it. When I'd first stepped into Cormac's shoes, everyone assumed I'd try to copycat him - cold, aloof, all business and badass. I'd kept the badass part, but that was all.

Where Cormac had been cold, aloof and all business, I was casual, and nonchalant...until you crossed me. That's where my temper took over and kicked into the badass. Occasionally, that same temper blocked out the logical thought process and I went from badass straight to dumbass. So far, I'd been able to keep those occurrences to a limited amount and the dumbass part of my persona was still, for the most part, flying under the radar.

"As everyone here knows, with the new additions and the continuous stream of refugees, we're running tight on room. I'd like everyone to go to their people and see if anyone is willing to double up. Also, I'm having a group go through the old casino shops and see which ones would be suitable for conversion into living quarters." The Lacard had once had a grand shopping mall inside its walls. Most of the store contents had been distributed to those in need and the surplus stored in the basements - now dungeons - for future use.

"What about food?" Adam asked, stepping forward. "This cold weather isn't going to help with the current shortages. All the leftover crops out there will be dead before we even get to them."

He stood there, arms crossed, and like everyone else, expecting me to solve all the issues like everyone else.

"The food isn't going to be an issue, at least for a while." And, not for the first time, I started to wonder when it had become my sole responsibility to clothe, shelter and feed these people. How much of the burden was I supposed to take? I didn't have any previous head honcho job experience, but was this really how this leadership thing was supposed to play out? Who would want this job? If I hadn't cracked up the world like a drunken teenager on a joyride gone bad, I'd have been out of there. But this was my equivalent to the crappy job you take until the damage is paid for and I'd stick at it until my debt was paid.

"How?" Adam asked.

"I won't say, but I'm working on something." I wasn't going to tell them that I'd sat down with Chip and zeroed in on the location of several canned food warehouses. If I did, there'd be nothing left by the time we got there.

Another issue we had was trust. While I was eating canned tuna and spam, a lot of people seemed to have some weird paranoia that I was dining on filet mignon every night, after I snuck up to the penthouse alone. I often wondered if it was because that is what they would do. Another reason I'd continue to drive the wrecked up car of a world.

"You need to be more open with us." Adam slammed a fist on the table.

"And you need to chill out." I waved my hand toward where he hit the table. "And save the dramatics, will you? I'm not sharing anything because I don't like when my plans are ruined and that's the end of it." I'd learned quickly to keep the important things to myself, after a food warehouse had been raided before we got there.

"After you stole from us, you owe us," Kaz said, the new top dog in charge.

I looked at him where he was sitting pretty close to me. Another issue with him gaining power was that stupid book. I knew he was riling up the wolves with tales - okay, maybe truths - about how Cormac and I had stolen from the wolves, working up the pack against me for purely political reasons.

"Yeah, a lousy boring book that was near to worthless."

"You don't steal from the wolves." He growled at the end of the sentence and I heard and answering growl from Dark, who I hadn't even realized had joined us.

I hopped off the table and grabbed the dictionary from underneath the shelves. I dumped it in front of him. "Here, we're even. Actually, you owe *me*, now, because this is probably better reading and a hell of a lot more useful." I walked away to his deep growl, and laughter from everyone else, as I stretched my legs in the front of the room. "Oh, and the person who wrote it could actually spell, too."

I saw the tell tale sign of Kaz's skin pimpling, a known indication of a werewolf close to the changing. But, for some reason, I didn't think he was really as mad as he was putting on. His face was too relaxed for someone who was supposedly in a rage.

If he wanted to continue this charade, I'd oblige him.

"Do you have a problem?" I walked back to the table again and rested a hip, leaned my head back and puffed out a set of four smoke rings. Except it wasn't smoke, it was pure magic, a new trick I'd been working on as I paced the halls alone at night.

Everyone watched the rings dissolve into the air with a bit of awe. Good, it was better if they were a little scared of me.

"No." His voice was low and I thought I saw a tic by the corner of his mouth.

"That's good. As the new leader of the wolves, I'll expect a list of names you'll be supplying for your portion of the work duty."

He nodded, his eyes still lingering in the air where the rings had disappeared.

"Now, does anyone else have something they need to discuss?" I searched the faces in the room. No one else spoke.

"Okay then, see you guys next week." Once I'd taken over, I'd instituted weekly meetings to try and stay on top of everything. It might not have been one of my brightest ideas.

"I'd like a moment alone," Kaz said, drawing my attention back to him.

I nodded toward the door, silently signaling for him to wait as everyone exited.

As soon we were alone, I leaned against the wall, not overly concerned. "What?"

He closed the six or so feet between us and leaned close, resting a hand by my head. "I heard you're rolling solo these days." Then the smile I'd seen him fighting lit up his face. He wasn't a bad looking guy, wolf man, or whatever. He definitely had the swagger that I unfortunately found so appealing, but my life couldn't handle another complication and I'd had one alpha too many crush my heart.

I didn't mean to insult him but I couldn't help but laugh. A death threat I would've expected. He joined in and laughed as well.

"Are you a schizophrenic, or is all that other stuff an act?"

"The wolves follow strength. In your face, ball breaking strength." He shrugged as if that was all the explanation necessary.

"Do you enjoy acting like that?"

"I don't really mind. Comes pretty natural to me. I'm sure as hell not letting anyone else make the choices I'll have to live by. So how 'bout it? You and me." He leaned slightly closer but didn't actually touch me, just hovered. "It's not even how hot you are. I've got hot chicks falling all over me on a daily basis. But girl, you've got bigger balls than my second in command. I bet you're a firecracker in bed, too." When he ran his knuckles over my cheek, I knew it was time to stop this little game.

"Thanks for the offer, but I don't think it's a good idea." I moved out from between him and the wall before he tried to touch more than my cheek.

I had to give him credit; he never lost his smile. He pushed back off the wall.

"Door's always open." He mimicked his words

with his actions as he opened the conference room door for me.

I nodded and then scrambled to put some space between us, not wanting any further display of amorous attention.

When I spotted Burrom at the end of the hall, I yelled down to him to hold up a minute as I walked briskly to catch up.

"Burrom, where are you heading?" Sneaky bastard always had something going on.

He paused for me and winked. "On my way to make the most of this fine body you helped me get."

"I need a minute."

"You willing to stand in if I get stood up?" he asked, smirking down at me.

Burrom flirting; I didn't know if I'd ever get used to it.

"Please don't do that with me. It's just..." I shuddered a little.

"Fine," he said, the gruff tones of the old Burrom sneaking back into the newly refined body. "What do you want?"

"I need to know something."

He looked at me and squinted his eyes, reading my expression.

"Not here," I added.

We entered the stairwell and made our way to his suite. A few other Fae had tried to take over Burrom's suite in his absence but had been swiftly given the boot. Unlike the wolves, none of the Fae, not even the new ones, messed with Burrom. Maybe it was the whole Ground Fae deal, or maybe it was something just unique to Burrom.

"What's up?" he asked as he sat and reclined against the sofa in his room. "And be quick about it."

I paced for a moment while he made faces and sighed loudly, hinting at his impatience to hear what was so important.

I stopped a few feet in front of him and finally just blurted it out. "I've been avoiding this conversation for a while, but it's time to clear up an issue. Would you have killed me out there, with the senator?" I'd been plagued by the memory of him threatening my life since we'd returned. I didn't know why, but, today of all days, I felt like I needed to know. Maybe it was just something in the air but truce with the senator or not, I felt like I was teetering on the edge of some sort of precipice. And the feeling was growing stronger.

He pursed his lips and looked at the ceiling for a moment.

"It shouldn't be that hard. Yes or no?" My hands rested on my hips.

"I'm thinking it through." He finally shrugged. "No. I wouldn't have."

"The length of time it took you to answer is a bit frightening and inspires little to no confidence."

I stared down at him, giving my *I'm highly disappointed* look. Since I'd taken charge, I'd realized it was crucial to have one of those looks in your repertoire.

"Hey, I had to make sure I was being honest." His palms were in the air as if he couldn't understand my issue with it.

"Can you lie? I've heard full Fae can't."

"Baby, I can lie like a rug. But I know you can tell a lie, so I was making sure of the accuracy."

"Will you be changing your mind, or can I depend on that answer remaining the same?"

"If I were the type to turn on you, which I'm not, I would have to say logically, my vested interests would lie with you anyway. So, even if I weren't the loyal sort, which I am, it wouldn't behoove me to join sides with the senator." He kicked his feet up onto the table and crossed his arms in front of his chest.

"Why not?"

"Forget the rest of the world for a minute. I'm not sure I would personally survive." He hooked a thumb in the direction of his chest.

"Why do you say that?" I didn't doubt he believed it, but I wanted to hear his rationale on the matter and see if there were any juicy tidbits I could tuck away for further use.

"Typically, when I go into hibernation, I'm restoring my power and vitality from the Earth's store of magic. I believe that I rose early due to you super charging the ground I rested in. Problem is, I don't know for certain if that was a power *give* or more of a power *lend*."

"So, in other words, if I go, you might go right back under?"

"Yes, and I'm not sure, if the senator is left to reign, there'll be much for me to come back to when I wake up fifty years from now. So, even if I didn't feel slightly indebted to you," he raised his fingers and pinched them together leaving the smallest gap just to demonstrate that he didn't owe me that much, "I certainly wouldn't want to die because of my own personal interests." He reached into his pocket and pulled out his pipe.

"What happened to the cigars?"

"I only smoke those in company."

Which I guessed I wasn't.

I looked at him and realized his concert shirts were back, just looking a lot snugger and a hell of a lot sexier than an ACDC shirt could look.

"So, I can count on you?" I was already exhausted by our air clearing.

"Hmmm, yeah, I guess you can say that I've learned where my bread is getting buttered." He let out a puff of smoke and I wondered where he was getting his tobacco these days.

"I'll take that as a yes."

"Let's get to the real matter at hand, shall we?"

"I thought I was, but please, share." I sat down on the other couch that was at a right angle from him, crossed my jean-clad legs and waved my hand.

"You're concerned that the senator's truce won't last. No matter how nicey nice he is acting, he wants something and he'll be causing problems in the future."

"That's your brilliant insight? I think every sane person living here is probably feeling like that." I pushed both hands through my hair as I stood up, wishing I could get rid of this feeling of foreboding. "I'll see you later."

As I walked out, a young pretty woman who used to deal in the casino walked in the suite.

Oh yeah, he'd better get my back.

Chapter Five

Uncomfortable Bedfellows

If I hadn't been so sleep deprived, I might have awoken more alert. My mind wouldn't have slipped back to that small window in time when Cormac being in bed with me was normal. I wouldn't have snuggled deeper in to the hard chest as the strong arm encircling my waist pulled me closer.

Then reality hit and I froze. It wasn't Cormac. And even if it was, it didn't matter.

My brain started to function and my limbs moved into action. Throwing off the arm, I jumped up, grateful that the room had been chilly last night and I'd worn sweats and a t-shirt to bed. I wheeled around to see who had climbed into bed with me and found Burrom. He was reclined against several pillows, resting his head on one palm, ankles crossed, a snug t-shirt showing off his body's much improved form.

"What are you doing?" I was angrier than I normally would've been at such a simple joke. But, for just a second, I'd thought it might be Cormac. The aching disappointment I felt in my chest fueled my anger; at myself, and at Burrom for provoking the unwanted feelings.

He gave me a dazzling smile in return with no

explanation.

"Burrom, what are you doing?" I repeated, my voice still harsh as I tried to shake off the reminder of things I'd rather forget.

He tilted his head and patted the bed next to him. He was sexy in a way that could melt a girl's bones; not surprising, since I'd somehow formed him in Cormac's likeness. If he could heal what was broken inside of me, I would've been all over him. But no matter how good he looked, I just wanted him the hell out of my bed. When someone rips your heart out of your chest, sometimes the damage is irreparable.

"Get up."

"Fine," he said in a bit of a sulk. "But you'd be amazed how this shit plays with the girls. Now I understand how Cormac got around so-"

"Please," I said, cupping my ears before he could continue, "there are certain things I don't want to hear about."

I walked into the living room, expecting Burrom to follow but not caring overmuch if he didn't. The penthouse was empty but for the two of us. Dark was supervising early morning guard duty. I knew because I'd made the schedule.

I went directly for the pot of coffee sitting on the counter. Burrom must have brought it with him. It was a sweet gesture and another unwanted reminder of Cormac. I'd never really paid much attention to the little things he used to do until they were gone.

"How did you get in, anyway?" I asked when Burrom came strolling into the room as I poured myself a cup and offered one to him. I used to like it light and sweet, but now I was happy to have it any way I could get it.

"I've got a surprise for you." Before I asked what, he plunked down a hazelnut nondairy creamer.

"Where did you get this?" It was rarer than a can of gasoline. With no cows nearby, nondairy creamer had become gold. And flavored? Forget it. I hadn't seen one of those in forever.

"I took a little trip to Bordertown."

Bordertown was the closest establishment near the tornado wall that did bartering with the senator's side. Something about the wall kept the rippers at bay and in turn drew all types of survivors of the shattering.

When he declined my offer to share coffee, I was secretly happy, not wanting to part with even a little bit of my new gift.

He settled himself into a comfortable position on the couch. "As to how I got in, I walked."

"I thought I locked it last night." Actually, I was positive I had not only locked the handle but also put down the monstrosity of wood that laid across the door. Paranoid much?

He smiled in answer and buffed his fingers on his shirt. "Locks mean nothing to me."

I took my cup of coffee to the opposite side of the couch and crossed my legs underneath me as I sipped, waiting to hear what had brought him here so early. He wasn't normally up before two or three in the afternoon.

The playful expression on his face turned serious. "Colleen has a fight at noon. I thought you'd want to know."

I rolled my eyes. Colleen was like my little sister, but a rambunctious, trouble making one. This would be the third fight she'd got into this month. One of these times I was going to kill her myself.

"With who now?"

"Another *changed*."

That might not be too bad. "Which one?"

"Evan."

"Evan has a nasty set of claws on him." I rose from the couch. I was going to need a refill of caffeine to get through this discussion, let alone the day, if this was any indication.

"I thought they were friends?"

Burrom raised his hands in equal bewilderment. "Death match?"

"When is it not with her? How do you want to deal with this?"

Fights were commonplace. We didn't have enough trustworthy people to police everyone.

When I initially tried to set up a police force, it quickly became apparent that they were just as likely to become abusive as protect. Not all of them; there'd been some great people that tried to do the right thing, but after a few too many complaints, I'd disbanded them and let the different factions have their barbaric justice. I needed to choose my battles. I also feared there would be fictitious complaints arising. If the masses were that intent on having blood, they would find a way and I knew I was defeated.

There was also the issue of what to do with someone if they did get caught? We had no judge, lawyers or even a jail. We had the dungeons, but not enough of them to house people for every transgression. It soon became obvious we were going to have to let everyone follow the wolves' example.

The only law set in stone was intentional killing, that happened outside of an agreed upon fight, would be met with execution. If you had a lesser grievance, one that perhaps didn't make you feel like mauling someone to death in a mindless blood lust, you could bring it in front of a panel of the heads of all the houses. If you couldn't solve it any other way, you could call the other party out for a fight. In those instances, if both parties agreed to fight to the death, it wasn't considered murder.

I tried to not get involved, but sometimes I

couldn't help it. I leaned my arms on the bar for a moment. I knew it was wrong. This was Colleen's fight and I should stay out of it. Finally, I nodded. Really, what was one more death on my conscience after so many?

"It might not work, be prepared for that."

"You pulled it off the last few times." Colleen was developing quite an impressive record in the ring, thanks in part to Burrom.

"Each person is different and will be affected to a different level. I can only do so much without showing my hand."

"I know." I remembered all the details clearly from when he initially explained it to me. He could apply a drag of sorts onto the opponent; as if their feet were being sucked into a mud pit, was how he explained it. It was an ability only a ground Fae could do undetected and only in small amounts, if we didn't want the other races to pick up on the scent of magic. Some of the *changed* were becoming very sensitive to the ebb and flow of magical power, so that was always a risk.

I knew he was sticking his neck out for me in these instances. The consequences of tinkering with a fight were never discussed. Didn't need to be. Everyone knew you'd be a dead man walking if you were ever caught. You wouldn't just be murdered, you'd be dragged through the streets, tortured and made an example of.

Even as head of this castle, or Burrom, head of his own group of Fae, we still wouldn't be able to avoid the heat that kind of tinkering would bring down.

I couldn't help but look questioningly at Burrom again. I still didn't feel wholly confident in his support of me when it came to the senator, and yet he'd do this for me. Was he just so confident in not being caught interfering, or was he not concerned about what would happen if he was? Burrom still had lots of secrets.

"On to other matters, I never told you about the last visit." I gave him a quick replay of my last meeting with the senator.

"I told you, I don't trust the senator's truce long term. I think you need to be as prepared as possible for the eventual outcome."

He eyed me up and down as I stood there in my too big clothes, my blond hair sticking out in all different directions from sleep. "But if I'm putting all my eggs in your basket," he stopped to make a gesture toward me, "this basket needs a little TLC."

"I just woke up!" I said in my defense and tried to push the hair out of my face.

"It's not what you look like. Well, not normally, anyway. We've got to get a handle on what your full abilities are."

"I know. I keep saying I'll make more time but then my days race by."

He looked at me again, trying to size me up on some level I didn't understand. "The trick at the meeting was neat, but a trick nonetheless. In pure potential levels, you're throwing off enough power to light up a city block, but I know you've no clue what to do with it."

"That obvious?"

He shrugged in answer. "You have to start testing it out and getting a handle on it. It doesn't help that everyone around here is too scared of the shit you can do so you can't get any hands on experience. They aren't looking to open up that can of worms. They'd prefer to pretend it didn't exist."

"And why is it that they're so scared?" For the most part, I'd tried to fly under the radar when it came to the general population. Then I saw him sitting there so smugly. "Did you start the rumors?"

"They aren't rumors if they're true."

"I'll take that as an admission of guilt."

"It's not all on me. You practically salivate at every confrontation. No one does that if they aren't carrying a little heat. Or no one that isn't a complete idiot, I should say."

"Colleen does and they take her challenge."

"Colleen might be rough around the edges and a natural born fighter, but it's not the same. Ever since Cormac left, you've had this look in your eyes that is akin to staring into your own death. Everyone knows you've got the ammo, I'm just not so sure you can shoot straight."

"You need a little polishing up too, by the way. Your delivery stinks." But his words concerned me. I knew in my gut for a while that sooner or later, it would come down to the senator and me. I remembered back to when I'd tried to confront him in his office, and he'd brushed me off. I hadn't known why, at the time. If I had just pursued him then, maybe none of this would've ever come to pass.

The *coulda, shoulda, woulda,* was about to hit hard if I kept up this train of thought. Why couldn't I ever dwell on the *did and was awesome* parts of my life?

"I'm starting to get some control." I took a deep breath and let out a stream of magical smoke, then reached a finger up to glide it along the tendrils.

"Jo, if we end up in a war with the senator, smoke rings aren't going to cut it."

"For today, just handle the Colleen issue. I'll handle my issues after I know we don't have to scrape her off the front courtyard."

He reclined back as he shook his head but didn't press the issue further. "You going to watch?"

"Nope." I never did when it was her, or someone I cared for. There was something all together unpalatable about seeing a person you liked getting ripped to shreds in front of you. To keep up appearances, I showed up to all the other fights. I didn't want to appear soft.

The door opening and closing in the foyer stopped any further discussion about Colleen. There was no one I'd trust with this information who didn't have blood on their hands.

"We've got about fifty new refugees downstairs," Dark said as he walked into the room.

The sheer numbers would be enough to draw my attention. Normally, refugees showed up in smaller groups; four or five, typically. I could see on his face there was more of an issue than just how many. "And?"

"One of them is Crash."

This got Burrom to his feet. "Do you think it's a trick?"

He asked the exact same thing I was wondering.

Dark, even in his human form, could smell pheromones and was an excellent judge of people because of it. Most of the wolves were. It was why when you went up against one of them, you'd better be sure of yourself. They could smell fear just like a dog, and it excited their instincts to attack.

"I think it's legit. He's asking to speak to you," Dark said, looking at me.

I nodded. "Send him up to the conference room."

"Do you want back up?" Burrom asked as Dark left the room.

"No, it's better if I'm on my own. I can handle him."

I left Burrom and made my way to the conference room, passing all different types of people, or what used to be people. Regular humans were becoming the minority. It was nothing to see someone covered in fur or a pair of wings these days. I secretly envied *changed* with wings. Even with my fear of heights, I'd drooled over a couple of nice sets of fluffy white feathers.

I reached the conference room before Crash and took a seat in Cormac's...No, it wasn't Cormac's chair. It was the chair at the head of the table. I closed my eyes, feeling too drained to hold back the memories today.

"Cormac, you've got to rest a bit." I grabbed his arm, trying to psychically drag him into the bedroom and force him to lie down. He'd been nonstop since the portal opened.

He didn't budge but looked at me.

"Jo, I don't need sleep anymore."

I returned his stare. He was holding something back. It was there in his pale eyes and what I'd glimpsed frightened me. I let go of his arm, taking a step back before I even thought about it. Whatever was going on was rattling him. I'd never seen Cormac like this and goose bumps spread up and down my arms.

"You're pushing too hard." That's all it was, I told myself. He was exhausted from the delusion that he didn't need to rest.

He looked at me and opened his mouth to speak, but hesitated. When he finally spoke, I wasn't sure if it was what he initially intended to say. "You're right. I'll slow down after I get everything settled."

Whatever I thought I'd seen in his eyes was shuttered now. Maybe it had never been there. I was so on edge myself, I was seeing things.

I pushed a boot against the conference table and sent the wheeled chair scooting backward. I should've demanded a real answer. If I had, maybe I could've fixed it. Maybe he would be here with me now.

We'd had sex the night before and I wish I'd known it was going to be the last time. Maybe if I'd said something different. If I'd told him I loved him, maybe he wouldn't have left.

I kicked the chair further backward trying to jar my mind along with my body. I had to stop. He'd known how I felt. I might not have told him, but I showed him.

He'd known. And it hadn't mattered.

The door swung open and my eyes shot to the figure of Crash walking in. I nodded to Dark, silently signaling him to leave us alone.

Crash was still as handsome as I remembered, with his sandy colored hair and hazel eyes. His smile was warm and friendly, but did nothing to diffuse the anger I still bore him. The senator had known the moment we'd crossed over into his territory. I'd expected it, but I thought he would have bought us a little time, not run straight to him.

"Jo," he greeted me.

"What brings you here?"

He walked a few feet into the room and I pushed myself back toward the table and kicked my legs up, crossing my ankles. He wasn't a threat to me and I wanted to make sure he knew.

"Me, and some others, have left the senator." He sat down, leaving a chair between us. It was a telling gesture that spoke of his unease.

"And now you want to stay here? Little late, don't you think?" I raised my eyebrows. "You torched that bridge pretty bad."

"I didn't tell the senator that you crossed. One of my men did. I wouldn't have done that but I warned you it was bound to happen."

"And is this person with you?" I might have to bump Colleen's fight at noon if he was.

"No. He stayed with the senator."

I couldn't stop the disappointment but I brushed it aside. "Why now? What's changed?"

"My daughter's dead."

The words took all the life out of the room and

instantly changed the mood. We both fell quiet and I digested the news. I watched the hurt flash in his eyes at having to speak about her. I could see the pain of her loss poke its head up at the mention and stab a fresh wound.

So many people were dead. I was all too familiar with how you could be walking along, managing to hold yourself together, until a simple memory caused you to seize in pain.

I wanted to act callously, as if I were immune to it, but I wasn't. Time made you better, but it never made you whole. Maybe if I hadn't just suffered my own loss it would be easier to shut down the empathy, but I was too raw myself. Cormac wasn't confirmed dead, but he might as well be. I hung my head as I tried to tamp down the compassion I couldn't seem to stop. So, instead of saying a lot of people are dead, as I probably should've, I said nothing.

"How many do you have with you?"

"I've got forty-eight now, but there might be more to follow." He looked around the room and then his gaze came back to mine, uncertainty there. "I told them I'd send word back if they were welcome."

"What do you have to offer?" Compassion or not, there could be no free rides, especially for a group such as this. I'd have a riot on my hands if I did.

"We're all ex-military and we didn't leave empty handed, either. We took a shit load of guns and ammo with us."

"We've got all the guns and ammo we need."

"Not this kind you don't." He smiled, knowing he had the ace in the hole.

When last we'd met, Crash's team had been in possession of ammo that Keepers, and rippers alike, were susceptible to. It was a game changer.

"How much?"

"Enough to clear out every ripper in Nevada about ten times over."

Now he had my true interest and I leaned forward.

"If this is true, why even bother with us? Why wouldn't you go stake out your own little piece of the wild west?"

"As peaceful as it is now, when it does get ugly, and we all know it will, I want to be standing next to the good guys."

I wasn't sure we were the good guys. Kaz ripping Rogo's head off didn't seem so good. There was nothing saintly about Colleen's fight with Evan, but I decided to let him think what he wanted. I needed those bullets.

"How did you get out? And what about the rest of them? How do I know they're going to be loyal and this isn't some sort of Trojan Horse? Are they all suddenly plagued by some new found moral compass?" I picked up a stray pencil that was lying on the table and tapped it, then twirled it in my hand while I waited.

"The senator hasn't been paying much attention since the truce, so getting out wasn't as hard as it might have been a few months ago."

"Everyone over there knows about the truce?" I feigned interest in my pencil baton act while he spoke.

"Not everyone. Just the upper tier, but they talk."

"You still didn't tell me why the rest of them want out."

He tilted his head down as if he didn't want to really speak aloud what he had to say next. "You know my daughter was the only thing keeping me there. I wasn't the only one whose family members could be counted among the *changed*.

"He uses them against us. Most of the people with me are good. They fought for their country out of loyalty and honor. Even the ones who don't have family didn't sign up with the senator because they thought he was evil. He told them you were the cause of the world's destruction. They believed him." He rolled his eyes, thinking to commiserate with me over the lies spread.

The pencil snapped in my hand. I took a deep breath before I continued, knowing it needed to be said.

"That's not all lies. I did have a hand in it."

He tapped his fingers on the table, needing a minute himself to formulate a response.

The drumming stopped. "It's true?"

I wanted to deny it, now that he was the one staring at me with condemnation. "The senator was the architect, but yes, I was directly involved. You could say I was the hammer he swung."

He nodded, taking another moment. "Did you know what you were doing?"

"No." The word rushed from me but I wouldn't beg for forgiveness, even though a part of me wanted to.

"I won't share that with my people."

"It doesn't matter. They'll find out. It's unavoidable."

"I'll deal with it then."

"Or I will." Which seemed more likely.

"Either way, I'd still like to stay."

As I looked at him, my obligation to the people already here warred with the desire to appease my guilt and welcome them with open arms. I wanted to try to right the wrong I felt I caused everyone, but I couldn't ease my conscience on other people's backs.

"We'll make room for now, on a probationary basis, and see how it goes." See if the current residents resent sharing the limited supplies and don't start challenging them to death matches. Or worse, risk the backlash and off them in their sleep.

He nodded and we both stood. I had to go figure out where I could squeeze fifty more bodies in. Crash, presumably, had to go talk to his men.

"I'm just warning you, though, if there are too many objections, you'll have to leave. And, so help me, if I feel like I can't trust you at any point, I will deal with the problem."

"You think you could?" He wasn't trying to start a fight but eyeing me up as a small female that couldn't handle him and his guys. His earlier unease seemed dulled by our calm conversation.

"I know I could. You should listen to the gossip. It's not all lies." I returned his smile but it didn't reach my eyes and I knew he felt the threat, and maybe as Burrom had suggested, seen his potential death staring back at him in my eyes.

"Who are you?" he asked, realizing, maybe for the first time, I wasn't the same girl he'd met months ago.

"I'm the product of my environment. And it's one nasty fucking world out there." I walked away, not offering any further explanation.

Chapter Six

Snow Day

I was taking Colleen and Chip on a little field trip with me today to collect food. Both had proven immune to the rippers. Colleen was an asset, with her ability to shoot electrical currents from her fingers, and Chip was logistics. He could get us wherever we needed to go by tapping into the satellites that still orbited the planet. With the map, he might not have been the best use of our additional person, but he was my first choice because he knew how to keep his mouth shut. I didn't want the adventure I was planning to be discussed.

I looked down at the map spread out in front of me. A red circle clearly marked the location of the canned food warehouse.

I folded and pocketed it, just in case Chip's wireless went on the fritz and made my way downstairs. Chip and Colleen were waiting for me at the door, dressed in camouflage as I was, even though I was ten minutes early. They smiled when they saw me and I wondered if I'd remembered to prep them on what we were actually going to do.

"Ready?"

"Beyond ready. We need to get the hell out of

this sardine can," Colleen said.

I nodded in understanding. Every day it seemed like there was less and less room and the tensions were escalating considerably.

We pushed outside, making tracks in the new snowfall. It had been snowing every day for the last week and I pulled the jacket tight around me as we headed out.

"The tensions might ease up for you, Colleen, if you stopped getting into fights."

In spite of the shiner she was sporting on her left eye, Burrom had reported back to me that Colleen hadn't needed any help fighting Evan.

"He had it coming. And I did take pity on him. I could've finished him off, but I let him live."

"I heard he begged for his life." The words caused bile in my mouth.

"A little." I heard the gloating in her voice and I wanted to shake some sense into her.

"There's nothing amusing about it." I grabbed her arm to get her attention. "And you aren't looking at the bigger picture. You think he's grateful now? Wait. That embarrassment is going to stew in his system until one day it poisons him with thoughts of revenge."

"I'm not worried. I can take him." Her bravado reminded me of my own youthful stupidity. I hoped she learned a little easier than I did.

"Only if you see him coming. And the ones you

do see coming aren't usually the ones that bring you to your knees. It's the stuff that hits you out of left field that takes you down." I let her arm go, hoping for her sake that she would wake up before she dug herself in too deep.

Neither of us said another word as we headed toward the truck we were taking. It was parked about five blocks away, right along the only clear path out of Vegas.

The truck was a huge neon blue semi and, for the first time, I really wondered if Colleen and Chip had been the best choice. I might have other things I wanted to accomplish, but we were also going to need to fill up that truck and none of us had much upper body strength.

I climbed up the steps and settled in. We'd already decided I'd do the first leg of the trip, then Colleen because she was a natural night owl. Chip would remain free to link into the satellites and bug out when we needed extra directional instruction.

It only took about five minutes for the heat to start warming up and we settled in as we headed toward the California border and our boon of canned food.

I found a comfortable position behind the wheel and adjusted to driving the monstrosity. Hotel California played in the CD player, thanks to Chip's forethought. It was a slow go initially, swerving the big truck through the cars abandoned in the more suburban areas. By time we'd hit the highway, the sun was already setting.

"When's Cormac coming back?" Chip asked, after we'd gone about a mile on the highway. Just like that, the cabin of the truck became my own little version of small talk purgatory.

"I'm not sure. He'll be back soon." I was starting to wish I could just pin that statement to my shirt.

"Where are the rippers?" Colleen wasn't looking at me but at the great expanse of snow covered desert. "It's getting dark and we're covering a lot of ground. I haven't seen one ripper."

I never expected talking about the rippers would be a pleasant topic of conversation but it beat out "Cormac, Cormac, and where's Cormac?" The lack of rippers should have made us all happy, but any disturbance in the norm these days had a tendency to set people's nerves on edge, including mine.

"Maybe with a lack of humans to eat, they're dying off," I replied. It was an optimistic thought, which is probably exactly why I didn't believe it. Optimists were a dying breed these days, and even way back when, before everything fell apart, I'd never been part of the happy rainbow tribe.

Feeling their eyes on me, I turned to look at Colleen and Chip.

"What?"

"You hitting the swill again?" Chip asked, leaning in close enough to smell my breath.

I pulled away from him with a scowl. "I can have positive thoughts."

"Leave her alone, Chip."

"Thank you, Colleen," I said but spoke too soon.

"If she's drinking again, I think I like her better this way. Let's not discourage her."

"Fine. I'm not full of booze, I'm full of shit. It's freaking me out, too." I pointed a free hand in their direction, "And, for the record, this is the last time I'm going to put out any effort for false optimism. It's a complete waste of energy if you two are going to refuse to drink the Kool-Aid."

I looked over at the two of them, hoping to see perfectly chastised faces. But they weren't looking at me. Their eyes were huge saucers and they both let out blood curdling screams. I whipped my head around to see a huge twenty-foot tall man ahead of us, just before we drove into him.

I slammed on the breaks and jerked the wheel to the right, which was probably the worst thing I could've done. Hey, it's not like I had truck driving experience. The trailer, even empty, added too much weight and kept pushing forward until the cab was jackknifed and the entire truck, with us in it, was thrown onto its side.

I'm not sure how long I was knocked out for,

but Colleen and Chip were still unconscious when I woke, piled underneath me like a lumpy bed. I was hoping they were only unconscious.

I took a deep breath and decided I should see if the giant was still there before I checked for pulses. If he was, it might not matter if they were alive anyway.

One of them moaned as I moved off them. "Sorry," I said to their limp forms as I tried to avoid stepping on them any further. The window was closed but at least it had a manual window opener. I pulled myself up and took a look in the direction of where he had been. He was gone but I knew that all three of us hadn't been delusional. He'd been there.

One issue hopefully gone, at least right now, but three more took its place. I had two unconscious *changed* in the cab of an overturned truck which was now smoking.

Ducking back into the cab, I knelt as close as I could without stepping on limbs.

"Chip? Colleen?"

I put my fingertips to Chip's throat first and felt a steady pulse. Colleen, much smaller than him, had unfortunately fallen onto the bottom of the heap, but had a steady pulse as well. She was sporting and egg sized bump on her forehead that was going to hurt like a son of a bitch when she eventually woke.

"Chip!" I tugged at his arm, trying to pull him off Colleen's chest in the crowded space.

Relief filled me as he groaned and I saw his eyelids start to flutter open. I tugged again and repeatedly called his name, trying to startle him out of his stupor.

"What the hell happened?" he said as he came to, groggily.

"We've got to get out of this truck. It's smoking."

I could see those words wipe the last of the haze from his expression.

"Shit," he said as he got a grip on our situation.

I pulled myself up and sat on the side of the open window, my legs dangling through the opening. "Can you lift Colleen and hand her to me?"

He stood awkwardly in the small space, his feet on the opposite door near Colleen's head. "You aren't supposed to move people who've been hurt. She might have a spinal injury."

"Chip, I need a little common sense right now. If this truck blows, she won't have anything. PICK. HER. UP." I looked at the smoke, now a dirty grey and thicker, coming from where the engine was.

He grabbed her and lifted her toward me. I repositioned myself, more dragging her out of the window, than lifting. Once Chip pulled himself out of the window, he tossed Colleen over his shoulder and we ran until there was a good fifty feet between us and the truck.

"You think this is far enough?" He started lowering Colleen to the ground, his breathing labored.

"I think-" My last words were muffled by the explosion of the truck. I yanked Chip down beside me as I crouched myself over Colleen, trying to block any shrapnel that might hit her. When nothing did, I looked at Chip. "Yeah, we're far enough."

"Is she okay?" Chip kneeled down next to where I was bent over Colleen.

"Colleen?" I lifted her head, and looked for blood.

"Am I dead?" she finally spoke.

"How do you feel?" I asked.

"Like I wish I was dead because someone's pounding a hammer on my skull." She reached out a hand behind her, seeking leverage to sit up. Chip moved forward and grasped her shoulder as I supported her back.

"What was that thing?" she asked, opening her eyes as she sat up.

"I don't know, but the truck's gone." The choking smell of the burning fuel drifted over to us, making it unpleasant to breathe deeply.

"Say it ain't so? Please?" She turned her head toward me where I was sure she could see the flames were still burning bright at my back. "Fuck. My. Life."

"I'm really sorry." And I was. It was biting cold

out. Chip looked like a wreck and I wasn't even sure if Colleen was going to be able to walk on her own. Her leg looked like it was bent at a very unusual angle compared to the normal way of things.

She leaned forward and shrugged. "Not your fault. I mean, when there's a big giant hanging in the road, what's a girl to do?"

"Now what?" Chip asked, looking at me as Colleen did the same.

"I don't think you are going to be able to walk," I said to Colleen. With all the stress of the moment, I wasn't sure she even knew how messed up her leg was, the adrenaline probably dulling the pain.

Her eyes watered as she looked down and saw the mangled looking mess that was now her knee.

I took point and moved down to her ankle, pulled the knife from my boot and slit her pant leg up to the knee. Nothing was bleeding or protruding through the skin but I had a horrible suspicion that if she stood up, her shin would be doing little more than dangling.

"It's just dislocated." I looked at her, trying to remain calm though I didn't feel it in the least. "It's not a big deal." Or wouldn't have been, when we had doctors and ambulances and all that other good stuff that used to exist. Now? It might be a big deal but I couldn't risk an emotional breakdown in the middle of the Vegas tundra.

I looked up from Colleen's malformed knee

joint to her face. Tears streamed down her cheeks in earnest.

"You're going to have to leave me here." She sniffed and ran her arm across her nose. "I get it. It's okay."

I wasn't sure if she was crying over the state of her leg or the nearing possible abandonment.

"We aren't leaving you here." We might all freeze with her, but we'd freeze together.

Chip was hunched down behind her shoulder, his face out of Colleen's view, which I was grateful for since his eyebrows were raised in disbelief of my words.

"Right, Chip?" I asked, forcing him to agree.

"Yeah. We're going to stay together."

I was glad Colleen couldn't see him roll his eyes and mouth a string of curses.

I looked around, seeing nothing but snow covered desert plains, and Colleen lying in a good ten inches of snow.

"We've got to get you up." I grabbed her one arm and motioned for Chip to take the other. "Sitting in the snow is going to make you lose body temperature quicker. I think." Between the two of us, we managed to get her up on her good foot, but she was grimacing. "Chip, plug in and tell us where the nearest structure is?"

"It's not exactly plugging in, it's more along the lines of-"

"Just do whatever it is you do?"

While his eyes glazed and his expression dulled, I took a look around. We were stranded out in the middle of nowhere and one of us was down a functioning leg. I pulled my funny phone out of my pocket but I already knew it was a waste of time. The phone lines were set up only in and around Vegas strip. Cormac's people hadn't gotten any type of towers erected this far. I'd taken over the situation after he left, so I knew exact distance away from the castle I could go, to the nearest block, before I would lose a signal. And getting a signal here would be akin to a miracle.

On the bright side, the giant was nowhere to be seen. Dark side, it looked like a small herd of rippers was heading our way, which wasn't going to do much for morale.

It wasn't alarming in the sense that any of the three of us were in danger. We all had enough magic coursing through us to be unappealing, as far as their menu went. But when those grey scaly bodies floated near, their eyes glowing yellow, it wasn't a really pleasant experience and not something you ever got used to.

Chips eyes came back to focus just as the small herd of five neared.

"Just splendid," he said sarcastically as he caught view of the rippers.

"So, how far is the nearest shelter?" Colleen's

body, even sandwiched between the two of us, had started to shiver. I was cold as well, but a bit better off than her.

"Our best bet is to head back toward home."

That wasn't what I wanted to hear. We hadn't seen a structure for miles and the last one had been a dilapidated gas station without an intact roof.

"Let's get going." It was going to be a long hike and I didn't want to dwell on how unpleasant it would be. I just wanted to get it over with.

We turned, Colleen hopping in between us as we started back. Since we'd left the casino earlier today, the winds had steadily kicked up into what seemed to be brewing into a very nasty snowstorm. With no food, and Colleen crippled in between us, I started to doubt we'd make it. I knew I had enough stamina to keep going the whole way back to the casino, but I wasn't sure about Chip making it a mile, let alone to the gas station. He was *changed,* but not in any way that seemed to improve his psychical prowess. Looking at his lean, gangly frame, I was a bit worried he wouldn't make it far at all.

We were carrying almost all of Colleen's weight, so her stamina wasn't an issue. If she wasn't clearly in so much pain, she could probably take a nap for all the help her one good leg hopping along seemed to provide.

We'd only moved about a quarter mile but we

were walking into the wind. My fingers felt frozen and my cheeks were burning with the cold. I could hear the gasps of pain Colleen was trying to swallow with every step. The rippers circled around us, mostly paying attention to me. At least they weren't making the pre-feeding hissing and clicking noises.

"Can you make them go away?" Chip asked, looking over Colleen's head at me.

Controlling them used some of the magic that flowed through me and it wasn't without a strain on my system. I hesitated, wondering if I should conserve my strength, but Chip's eyes were pleading, and I took pity on him.

"Okay." Just before I was about to utter the words which would hopefully get them away from us, I stopped, an idea forming. "Hear me out before you say no," I said to them. "Chip, how far away are we from any type of shelter?"

"I can't say exactly without connecting back in but about fifteen miles?" His teeth were starting to chatter, and I had to concentrate in order to understand him.

"And would you say the storm seems to be kicking up and the temperature dropping?"

Colleen looked at me, eyes squinting. "Is this supposed to be a pep talk? Cause it sucks."

"Just listen, would you both agree that there is a good chance of at least two of us getting frost bitten?"

"And it just keeps getting better and better. I'm really glad you don't have children," Colleen continued.

"I'm going to see if I can get the rippers to take us home," I said, waiting for their reaction.

"What?" they both asked in unison

"Look at them." I pointed to the creatures as they circled us. "They glide over the snow. I've seen them move at what has to be close to forty or fifty miles per hour."

"Even if you can make them do it, what if they eat us?" Chip asked.

"They don't like our meat."

"I don't like this," Colleen said.

"You two are going to have to decide what you dislike more, riding with rippers, if I can even make them do it, or having your fingers and toes snapping off."

Chip moaned at my words, or maybe just the image it provided.

Colleen looked over at me again, "You really think you can do this?"

"I'd give it a fifty-fifty shot. My guess is they'll either do it or not, I don't think they'll try and eat you. So now it just depends on how much you want to keep your extremities."

"I'm in."

"Colleen, you are so easy," Chip complained.

"First it's the wolf and now this?"

"The wolf?" I asked.

"Because I don't want to lose my toes? You're just a big wimp," Colleen shot back. "I'm trying to live my life and I suggest you do the same."

"Which wolf? Forget it, I don't want to know. We all have to agree on doing this. No one gets left behind. All or nothing." I paused, my toes freezing in my thin boots. Why hadn't I worn gloves? Duh, stupid question. The Vegas strip didn't have too many winter wear stores to salvage from. I was grateful I had a down ski jacket.

Colleen turned the full blast of her temper on Chip. "You either do this or I tell Sharon you've got a thing for her. And if I lose my toes because you're a wimp, I'll zap yours off while you're sleeping!"

"No, you would not!" Chip said, dropping Colleen's arm from around his shoulder and effectively dumping her weight onto me. I sidestepped as I was forced to take up the slack.

Colleen hopped, almost knocking me over in the process. "Oh, yes I will! I'm very attached to having my little piggies!" she screamed back at him.

"Chip, Colleen will go first. If they don't eat her, will you try it?" I asked, looking for a compromise.

He studied the rippers hovering nearby. I saw him shudder before he turned back to us. "Fine. Her first."

"Okay, Colleen, you ready?"

Her face whipped to me. "I figured you'd go first?" All her former temper instantly disappeared into a childlike innocence.

I didn't want to admit that I detested the idea of being held by a ripper with equal vigor or I'd never get them to go along with the plan.

"Chip, grab her arm."

He stepped back over and the two of them seemed to be at peace again now that I was going to be the sacrificial lamb. I'd quickly learned being leader sucked but I had no idea to what extent until right this very second.

I didn't know how literally they took instruction so I decided to do it one step at a time. I still wasn't even sure how they understood what I was saying. It's not like I heard them chatting in English over a cup of tea, and I didn't want one of these creatures to grab me and take off, leaving Chip and Colleen sitting in the snow, stranded.

"You," I said to one of the bigger ones. "Pick me up."

The thing started to glide over to me, tilting its head this way and that.

I waved it closer to me, trying to encourage it. It reached a clawed hand out toward my arm but withdrew it and screeched loudly the second it made contact. It backed up quickly, cradling his hand, claw, whatever you called its weird appendage.

"Please don't make it try that again. I don't think my eardrums can take it," Chip said.

"I wonder why it can't touch me?"

"Oh well," Chip said, thinking this experiment was over.

I didn't budge as I kept my eyes trained on the rippers, sizing up the next largest one. "It doesn't mean they can't carry one of you."

Before either of them could protest, I directed my next choice to pick up Colleen. The thing swooped in and grabbed her around the waist. She yelped as it lifted her and ignoring her current squealing, I ordered another one to grab Chip.

They both squirmed uncomfortably in their escort's arms. The rippers didn't appear to be happy, either. Their expressions didn't change but they held both of them out at arm's length.

"How do they even know what you're saying?" Chip asked.

"I don't know."

"We can't go. What about you?" Colleen asked, frantic about the next order I was going to give the rippers.

"I can heal, you can't. Go, get another truck and come back for me."

They would've argued but I looked both rippers in the eyes, uncomfortable as that was, and said, "Take them to the big building where I live."

Colleen and Chip were yelling for me to stop

but I ignored them, as did the rippers. And then they were disappearing into dots on the snowy horizon.

I sighed, watching the vapor of breath disappear into the cold air and looked around. "I guess it's just us, boys," I said to the rippers left lingering around me. I took my first step forward alone, my ripper entourage keeping pace.

I didn't check the time as I marched ahead. The winds picked up and a fine hail stung as it hit my face. The snow was falling so heavily I could only imagine this must be a blizzard. I'd grown up in Vegas; I'd only ever seen snowflakes that melted as soon as they hit the ground.

I now realized the importance of so many things that I used to take for granted. News people, screaming about a storm coming a week beforehand, always seemed a bit of an irritation. Now look at me, stranded in a blizzard.

When I tripped over my own feet, I knew I was in bad shape. Hypothermia was kicking in. I'd stopped shivering, another bad sign.

I scanned the horizon as best I could in the low visibility. All I wanted to do was rest for a tiny bit. I knew it was the last thing I should do, but I was only going to stop for a little while. Just to rebuild my strength and let the worst of the storm pass, then I'd get up and start walking again.

I saw the shape of a car, its form partially hidden by the thick blanket of white. I pushed the snow away and the door creaked open on the interior of an older Toyota Corolla. I climbed onto its fabric seats.

It took a few minutes to pull the door shut over the fallen snow that blocked it, but I finally tugged it closed and curled up into a ball in the corner to take a short nap. I knew I couldn't stay in here long, they'd never find me, but I just needed a few minutes to rest.

Chapter Seven

Return of the King

"Jo, you've got to wake up."

I heard the voice; I just chose to ignore it. I didn't want to wake up as it so loudly suggested.

"Jo, wake up," the deep husky voice repeated. Actually, it sounded more like a command. I ignored it anyway.

Part of me registered that I was being pulled from my resting place in the backseat of the Toyota by rough hands and I tried to swat them away but to no avail.

"Get off." The hands ignored me as I was dragged the rest of the way out. I wanted to go back to sleep. I'd never felt so tired in my life but he wouldn't leave me be.

He lifted me out and was carrying me across the snow somewhere. My head rested in the crook of his neck, nestled close to his heat. I recognized the scent of his skin and without conscious thought, snuggled closer to him.

Cormac.

He juggled me while opening the door to an SUV and climbed into the front seat. He played with the buttons on the dashboard and the warm toasty interior was suddenly being blasted with enough heat to create a sauna.

"Cormac?" My mind was still trying to wrap around his presence but he wasn't looking at me; he was unbuttoning the shirt under his jacket.

Then his hands were on me, pushing my jacket open.

"Stop." I pushed his hands away but he tugged my shirt up anyway and pulled me close to him. My legs straddled his hips, bent at the knees. I faced him where he reclined against the seat, our naked skin, flesh to flesh along the front of our torsos.

The fog started to lift from my brain. I tried to pull away from him in earnest but his arms were wrapped around me, holding me snug to him.

"Get off me," I said, having a hard time talking with the way my teeth were chattering.

"I can't." His voice whispered near my ear as he continued to hold me to him.

My thoughts slowly started to clear as I sat there with him. Cormac was here. I wanted to curse him out but I couldn't stop shaking. I didn't know if it was from the cold or the emotions roiling inside me.

I wanted to know why he was here. How he'd found me? Was he coming back or was he on his way somewhere else? But I was afraid if I spoke I'd fall apart.

I lay there, pressed against him, secretly relishing it. I had to, because this would be the last time I'd allow myself to be this close to him.

I knew why I was silent, even as the shaking subsided, but I didn't know why he was. If he planned on staying, shouldn't he have been rattling off excuses and platitudes? Did his silence mean he was leaving?

We stayed like that for a while and I felt one hand slowly rubbing up and down my spine underneath my jacket. I closed my eyes for a minute, pretending he hadn't left for months without word, but it was a dangerous game and I knew where it would lead. More heartache. I took a deep breath, preparing myself for what I needed to do.

I don't know if he sensed my mood or felt me stiffen, but his hand stopped moving. I pushed against him. He didn't give in right away, still holding me tight to him, his head leaning close to mine and buried in my hair. I heard him take a deep breath, and then the pressure of his hands changed.

He gripped my waist and lifted me off him, then slid away and took the seat behind the steering wheel. I pulled my shirt down, facing away from him, before I settled into the passenger side.

"Where are you driving?" I asked in an accusatory tone as he put the truck in gear. I'd become completely disoriented and with the snow whipping around, I didn't know if he was driving toward the castle or away from it. He might be willing to abandon everyone, but I wouldn't.

He looked at me. This was the first time I'd seen his face in months. I don't know why I expected to see something different there, but it was the same deep set pale eyes that had always been able to undo me.

"To the casino." He looked back toward the road, or what could be seen of it underneath the snow.

"I hope you don't plan on staying."

"I do."

"You're not welcome there anymore." And I don't think I could see you every day and hold it together. I'd thought I'd locked you away in a nice and neat compartment in my brain, and here you are, rattling the chains so easily. I could already feel myself being torn apart. As much as I hate you, I want to reach over and cling to you for dear life, begging you not to leave again.

"Well, that's unfortunate for whoever objects, since it's still my casino." He was smiling as he said it, as if the idea of someone telling him to get out of his place made him want to laugh.

"I object." The idea of him strolling back into our lives enraged me. Or maybe it was because I felt like a bundle of raw emotions and he was acting blasé.

The smile fell from his face and he stared back at me.

"I didn't want to leave. I had to."

"For such a dire need, you seem quite unchanged." I made a show of eyeing him from the top of his thick black hair to the rugged boots on his feet.

"I needed to go." His voice was strained as he said the words.

"I don't believe you." I stared straight ahead.

"Why? When have I ever lied to you?"

"I don't want to hear the bullshit. Obviously you worked out whatever little problem it was. It must have been horrible."

"So that's how it's going to be? I don't know why I thought you might have grown up."

"Did you think it would be anything else, after you walked out? Did you think I'd be one of your little girlies, just thrilled to have you back paying attention to me? Why am I being like this? Because I *have* 'grown up.' I've been taking care of things while you were gone."

"I told you. I had to."

"So, what horrible things happened? Did you go on some murdering rampage?"

"No." His jaw was tense and he wasn't looking at me either now.

"Did the magic make you rape and pillage entire villages or some other equally evil deed?" I arched a sardonic brow.

"No, but that doesn't mean…"

"Then like I said, save it."

I turned my face toward the window, signaling that I was done speaking to him, but he kept going anyway.

"I know you. You're upset but you'll get over it."

I wasn't sure if he said it for me or himself. I didn't respond. I wasn't interested in talking this out with him. He'd made his choice.

When we finally pulled up as close as we could to the castle, my hand paused on the truck door handle and I felt a burning need to disabuse him of his conclusions. "You're wrong on both points. You don't know me, not anymore, not who I am now. And I won't just 'get over it.'"

I didn't wait for a response but hopped down out of the truck. Partly I rushed because I was dying to get away from him and clear my head. But mostly, I was afraid if he pushed me, I'd collapse into his arms and beg him to stay.

I ran ahead, but he wasn't too far behind. He was close enough, in fact, that I could hear the warm welcome of cheers that went through the castle at his entrance. I didn't stick around long enough to listen to the hoorays and happiness as his presence churned up muddier waters within me.

When I stepped into the penthouse moments later, I saw Dark and Dodd there. I told them their boy was back, with an extra added reminder to keep to the storyline. Even knowing the truth of what I considered his betrayal, they practically trampled me to get out the door and get to Cormac as quickly as they could.

The king was home, and apparently, I was the only person who wasn't overjoyed.

Chapter Eight

Long Live the King

"Someone just dropped this off for you," Kever thrust a note at me and rushed past on his way to seek out Cormac.

"Wait! Have you seen Chip and Colleen?"

"Yeah, they're with the Fae doctor. They showed up unconscious on the stoop a few hours ago babbling about giants. She had to sedate them."

"Are they okay?"

"She said they'd be fine." His eyes kept darting down the hallway in the direction of where everyone was heading.

I grabbed the note and told him, a bit impatiently, to go. He was off before I got another word out.

I fingered the thick paper with a wax seal. Pocketing the note, I hurried back to the penthouse. I'd have some privacy, since it would take a while for Cormac to make his way through the throng of admirers. I broke the seal but already knew who had written it.

I need to speak with you. Meet me at two a.m. in front of the ruins of New York.

I didn't need a signature, not that he'd bothered. It was from the senator. I also understood he meant the ruins of the casino, not the city. Besides not having any possible way of getting to the east coast in twenty minutes, there were no ruins to mourn the loss of that historic place.

I threw the note into the fireplace, wondering who was to thank for the blazing flames. I grabbed my jacket and left the penthouse without a word to anyone and headed back out into the frigid weather.

When I got there, the senator was standing alone in front of the ruins of a casino that used to be one of the main attractions on the Vegas strip. Wrapped in a black mink, his blond hair cascaded down his back as his gaze wandered over what was left of the building.

"You summoned me?" It wasn't a question so much as a sarcastic statement.

"You know, I didn't want it to be like this." He motioned toward the destruction. "I didn't have a choice." His voice, always cultured, sounded softer than usual. As if he really did regret the chaos he'd wrought, and disliked caring about it even more. "I wouldn't have done it if they'd given me any other choice. But no. There was no speaking to them."

I knew "them" was the Keepers. It was horrible to know he and I shared this link, this mutual regret and responsibility for something so horrific. He might have been the designer but I had completed the plans.

"Why did they banish you?" I waited, wondering if he would reveal what had happened so long ago with the original Keepers. It was a history not even Cormac truly knew.

He let out a long sad sigh before he finally spoke. "They couldn't control me. They thought they could create me and then I would do whatever they wanted. They weren't prepared for me to have my own desires. They wanted me to be a slave. When I wouldn't, they banished me to a dimension that is unfathomable to most humans. Imagine a thousand years among creatures like the rippers and worse. I was doomed to living eternity in a living nightmare." He looked at me, lids lowered. "When someone has a child, shouldn't that child be able to become their own person?"

I didn't want to feel for this creature, whatever he truly was, but I found that I suddenly did. He seemed so human right now, in his beautiful form. Then I remembered Rick and his senseless death at the café, the needless murder just to make a point. The senator played the victim, but I knew better. He killed and took without a qualm. He wasn't the victim.

I didn't have a safe answer and didn't want to get dragged further down the rabbit hole, with its morally confusing twists and turns, so I changed the subject.

"Did you bring the rippers to this world?"

"No, not I." The corner of his mouth twitched and I knew he was holding back some information.

"What did you want to speak with me about?"

"I've heard Cormac has returned." He gave me his full attention then and the look I saw in his face sent a tremor through me before I could get a hold of my reaction.

Why such rage? What did it matter to him?

"Yes." There was no point in lying. I was sure the spies were quite up to speed after Cormac's grand entrance although it was quite unnerving that he'd found out this quickly. We'd barely just returned.

"How did you know?"

"You think you are the only one I watch?"

"Is that going to cause a problem with our agreement?"

"Why should it?"

He was lying. I involuntarily went to move a step back but stopped myself. I didn't want the senator to know I was aware of his true feelings, or worse, that I feared him. When he didn't continue, I asked, "Is that all you wanted?"

"I know he has sway over you." It was a condemnation.

"You're mistaken. I do exactly what I want." I watched him as he took in my reply. For something wholly inhuman, he had very mortal reactions. His brow furrowed and his eyes seemed to sink deeper. I had a strange feeling, that regardless of what he said, this would be the day I'd mark down on my calendar that our truce had ended.

He didn't speak again but simply walked off. I watched his back retreat, knowing somewhere deep inside, all hope of peace was disappearing with him.

I sat by the ruins after he left, trying to convince myself I was wrong. When I couldn't after an hour, I gave up and headed back to the castle, the feeling of impending doom stronger than ever. I'd almost made it back when the lightning bugs appeared.

"Jo." They sang my name out like usual.

"What are you guys doing out here tonight? Don't you have somewhere warm to bed down?"

"We have to talk to you, Jo."

"What's wrong?" I asked, pausing about a half a block before the castle.

"We're hearing strange things."

"Strange how?" I couldn't wait to find out what would seem odd to talking lightning bugs

"He's coming. Gotta go."

I turned to look but I already knew who they meant.

Cormac was walking toward me with a purposeful stride as the bugs were already zipping down the block. I started walking forward, not toward him but to the castle.

It was impossible not to have him in my vision as he approached from the direction I was headed but I probably would've watched him regardless. Everything about him drew me in. The way he moved jarred loose buried memories. The way his body felt, moving over mine. His hands wrapped around me, pulling me still snugger to him as he had relentlessly drove deeper. His desire stripping down everything I was, all my pretenses, until nothing was left but pure need. Claiming. Being surrounded by the unleashed intensity that was him, normally so controlled, it swallowed me whole as I'd bathed in the force of who he truly was on a primal level.

I'd felt the full force of him, had succumbed to his raw appeal. And I'd relinquished everything I was. I'd laid myself bare to him in those moments, and he'd accepted and relished in everything I offered.

How do you step back from that? How was I supposed to be near him and be less? I'd let him in and now I didn't know how to keep him out.

I felt the flush of my skin even as I told myself to keep my distance. My brain screamed to stay away but my body, maybe even my soul, craved his nearness.

"Where've you been?" he said as we approached each other. He didn't touch me but stood so close, as only someone intimate would. His eyes moved over my face and then seemed to fixate on my lips.

"Out." It was curter than I'd intended but my emotions were throwing my senses into turmoil.

"I can see that."

I went to move past him; I needed distance. I wasn't ready for this, whatever it was.

He stopped me with a hand on my arm when I would've kept going. "With who?"

"I'm not your concern." I yanked roughly away from him and he let it go.

"Whether you care to acknowledge it or not, everything that happens here is my business. I deserve to be told what is going on."

I'd planned on telling him. He did need to know but his demanding, his strolling back in here after months away, sent my temper into a flare.

"That you gave up. I've been the one keeping things together for the last few months while you ran off to deal with your issues." I made a point of looking him up and down as I said this. "Issues that didn't seem to be much of anything, from the look of things."

"This is still my place."

I threw my hands up. "You're right. It is. And if I do something that concerns this building, I will make sure to consult with you. But I'm not. My business isn't yours. Stay out of my life. Don't have people keeping tabs on me. And don't worry about how I'm doing. I can take care of myself."

"It doesn't have to be like this. You're overreacting."

I shrugged and crossed my arms. "Fine. Go ahead. Explain."

"I was afraid of what I'd do if I stayed. I was afraid I'd hurt you."

"Because you went so crazy? Yeah, I remember now. You look like you really went through the wringer while you were gone." It was an absurd statement, considering he was glowing in good health.

"I didn't know what I'd do."

"You were so afraid of hurting me but leaving was the most hurtful thing you could've done."

"Why are you being so stubborn?"

"Cormac, it's over. You and I are done." I just had to try and convince myself as hard as I was trying to convince him. Because I felt a lot of things right now: raw, hurt, crushed. But nowhere, in all of the emotions swirling to the surface, did I feel even the slightest bit finished.

I turned and headed into the castle with Cormac on my heels when it hit me, we were both headed to the same place.

I continued to walk even though I had no clue as to what I was going to do and Cormac continued to follow me. I wrenched open the door, and the smiles of the guards as they looked at Cormac with hero worship just made me more agitated.

I made it to the penthouse, Cormac silently following. When I walked in, and saw the door to the guest bedroom open, I remembered Dark had guard duty at the side entrance tonight. It was a relief to be able to fight this out in private, if it that was what it was going to come to.

I watched Cormac walk into the living room and relax onto the couch, like time had stood still. He'd already changed into his white shirt and pants and looked just like he had before he left.

"You need to find a new place to sleep." I tried to avoid looking at him as he folded his arms behind his head and crossed his ankles.

"Can't do that." His voice was in complete control again. Any weakness he'd shown outside was walled off. He was digging in and I could battle him or not, but I knew him well enough to know he'd set his course.

"Why?"

"Because you told everyone I was out searching for a place for them while I was gone. I've since informed them that this still seems to be the best location, which, by the way is truthful. How do I explain getting booted from *my* penthouse after returning?"

"I don't care. Make something up. I'm not giving up my bedroom."

"And even if I were willing, which I'm not,

where would I go? This place is packed tighter than a sardine can."

"I don't care. You found somewhere to sleep for the last three months, go back there."

"No." He managed to shrug somehow while he was reclined.

"You gave it up. It's mine." I knew it was useless. Why was I even bothering? He wasn't going to budge.

He made a loud show of yawning as he stretched and got up.

"You aren't sharing my room," I said, seeing where this was heading and walked into the bedroom first, shutting and locking the door before he could come in.

"If you refuse to leave, you can sleep on the couch," I yelled it through the door. "And besides, when the hell did you start sleeping again, anyway?" I didn't get a response but was too chicken to open the door back up and see how he was reacting.

I collapsed on the bed, prepared to be awake for the rest of what was left of the night, knowing Cormac was on the couch. I fell asleep not two minutes later.

Chapter Nine

Bunkmates

I felt the arm around me, the body against my back and I stirred. The arm tugged me closer into its warmth.

"Burrom, I told you-" my brain kicked into gear just as Cormac's yell filled the room.

"Burrom?" he roared as he leapt from the bed as if it had burned him. I hoped no one was in the living room. Maybe the whole floor, 'cause he was loud, and also gloriously naked.

"Shhh! I don't want anyone to hear you."

"That you're fucking him?" He didn't bother lowering his voice.

I heard a noise by the bedroom door right before I heard Dark's voice. "You're fucking Burrom?"

I was out of bed with one hand on my hip and another pointed at Cormac. "See?"

Cormac, ignoring me, turned to inspect the stone wall and the wooden door.

"Dude, the walls aren't sound proof anymore," Dark said from the other side of the door. "We've got more of the vintage acoustics these days."

Cormac stopped by the door and swung it open. "Dark, you've got five seconds to get the hell out of the penthouse."

I couldn't see Dark's face, all I heard was. "Dude, you got it. All you had to do was ask."

Cormac slammed the door shut.

He stood unmoving, looking like he might burst a vein as it throbbed in his neck.

"I'm not sleeping with Burrom," I said in hushed tones, not because I thought he deserved an answer but because I wanted to shut him up.

I toyed with the idea of letting him think I had been sleeping with Burrom, just for a little payback, but it wasn't worth the strife it would cause. I didn't want the entire place to think I was messing around with him. I knew there were already rumors, with the amount of time we spent together.

There were other entanglements I'd prefer not to have any light shed on and it would be a lot harder if the entire castle was watching us all the time.

But that didn't stop me from adding, "Not that you have any right to care or say anything about it if I did."

"He's out of here. Today."

"No, he's not."

He wasn't screaming anymore. He hastily threw on his pants and walked out of the bedroom.

"Shit, can I ever wake up in peace anymore?" I ran out of the bedroom after him and had to go all the way into the hall before I caught up. At least he wasn't disappearing.

"Stop," I yelled at him as he was opening the door to the stairwell, but he didn't listen to me. I rushed forward and grabbed his arm. I stepped in front of him, psychically blocking his way. He could have easily pushed passed me but he paused.

I dropped my hand quickly, self conscious of touching him, of what being this close to him did to me.

"I need him here. Even if I had slept with him, which I didn't, I couldn't allow you to kick him out. It's bad business."

He stared down at me, trying to read my face.

"I didn't sleep with him."

I saw his pulse start to slow.

I knew Cormac. When he didn't move forward and I saw the gleam in his eye, I took a deep breath in preparation for what was to come.

He took a step back from me, the last thing I expected, and leaned a shoulder against the wall, crossing his ankles. Whatever had happened to him out there, one thing was obvious: he was still pure Cormac.

"Why do you want to keep Burrom here? If it's business, like you say, then tell me why you need him."

It galled me after all this time to have to explain anything to him but he had the entire castle at his back. If he wanted Burrom gone, he'd get it.

So I pulled out my trump card. I needed to tell him anyway.

"I think my truce with the senator is at an end. We're going to need him."

"Doesn't mean he has to live here," he said.

"You aren't worried about the senator?" I'd expected a stronger reaction, at least something. Cormac wasn't the type to run around screaming the sky was falling, but I'd expected more than this.

"We always knew he wouldn't be held at bay for long."

Plan B, "Well, there are other reasons. Burrom allows me an edge with certain things."

He shook his head. "Not good enough."

He pushed off the wall and started toward the staircase again. I wasn't sure if he was bluffing or not, but I didn't want to take the chance.

"Stop! It's in both of our best interests for him to be here, but I can't divulge the details."

He stopped again, this time right next to me.

"With the fights."

"How did you know?"

"I was catching up yesterday while you were hiding from me and going to clandestine meetings."

"I wasn't hiding. And you don't know anything." Burrom never would've told him, and besides me, no one knew.

He smiled and continued. "I know about the fights. Not pretty, but I understand it. I also heard about some of the match ups. Colleen couldn't have taken some of them without a little help.

"From there it was obvious who would be willing and able to help."

"So you agree, he stays," I said, but might have relaxed too soon.

"I don't like his tinkering. So no, I don't agree."

"Colleen would be dead."

"But it's right that she killed others? Unfairly?"

"She didn't kill Evan."

"It's not right."

"Well, I don't care, because Burrom's staying."

"I don't agree with the manipulation. I didn't say I wouldn't agree to him staying, just that I don't like the tinkering. In times like this, honor is more important than ever. I don't want him manipulating fights, but I won't insist on him leaving, on one condition."

"What?"

"We share the penthouse."

I chewed on my lip, thinking over my options. If I didn't agree, how was I going to get around him?

"You don't have any other options."

I shook my head. It was an obvious deduction on his part but it still grated on my nerves, maybe more so because he was right. I still couldn't take him on and I knew it.

"Fine. We share the penthouse."

"And, Jo," he put his finger under my chin, tilting my head up when I would've ignored him. "No more tinkering. My orders."

I jerked my face out of his grip and returned the favor by gripping his chin. "You don't rule the roost here anymore. You need to realize that."

He grabbed my wrist before he kissed my knuckles and let it go. He laughed, amused at my actions and turned his back on me as he strolled to the penthouse.

"We shall see who 'rules the roost' sweetheart," he said, right before he walked in.

I was the one staring at the walls and screaming now.

Chapter Ten

New Friends

I was lying on the couch with an arm thrown over my head when Colleen walked in, her leg in an ugly cast. I'd slept there last night, when Cormac refused to leave the bedroom. It irritated me to no end considering he didn't even need to sleep anymore, and I was positive he was just faking it all night long. Score one for him. We were now tied for one night each claiming the bed. One him, one me. I had no intention of losing to his fake snoring tonight. Big jerk didn't even know that he didn't snore.

"How's your leg?"

"Sucks. What's wrong with you?" She sat down on the end of my couch, smushing my legs, instead of opting for the empty one across from me. I knew she had a cast and all but there was all sorts of empty seating. Was it really necessary for us to sit together? People hogging my bed, now people hogging my couch. Did nobody appreciate personal space?

I'd never wanted a sister but I had a feeling this was what it would have been like. If someone other than her had walked in, I would've at least put on a show of not being depressed.

"I'm not fun anymore," I said.

"Forgive me for asking, but did you used to be? That must have happened before I knew you."

I lifted my arm just enough to make sure she could see my scowl.

"Scowling at me doesn't magically rewrite the past."

"Fine, maybe I wasn't fun, exactly, but I was funny."

"Okay, I'll give you that one. As much as I'd like to sit and wallow with you, I'm only here to deliver some correspondence."

I hadn't noticed the paper in her hand until then. The yellow crayon told me who it was from before I even read it.

Meet us out front at sundown.

"The bugs?"

"Yeah, how'd you guess?"

"Can't they find a pen?"

"I think they like the colors."

"So, are you getting up? What the hell is wrong with you, anyway? I figured you'd be nauseatingly happy now that your man is back. I planned on avoiding you for at least a solid week, until the edge wore off. You should've told me it was safe."

"Seriously? My happiness would've been that irritating to you?"

"I feel like the right thing in this situation would be to lie, but yeah, it would've been God awful. I might have even had to fight someone to take the edge off all that sunny joy overflow, even with the cast."

"Well then, you will be relieved to know I'm not overjoyed and have no plans for an abundance of happiness in the near future."

"Thank God! But why?"

I'd been lying to them for months, so I couldn't exactly come clean now. I decided to keep it brief. "We had a fight."

She didn't pester me for information, just nodded. In this way, Colleen was old beyond her years. She instinctively knew when to leave a subject alone.

"So," she said, just nodding.

"Yep, not to worry, no rainbows and flowers here. Not even a stale piece of crumbling chocolate."

"Are you getting up anytime soon?"

"What is soon?"

"I don't know, next day or so?"

"Oh yeah, I got that covered. Got a date with some bugs, even if Cormac is running around stealing my job."

"Okay then, have a good sulk. I'll see you later."

"See ya," I said as she limped out of the room.

Regardless of my intentions, I got up shortly after she left, anyway. Staying in the penthouse was just asking for constant contact with Cormac, as he was always in and out.

I spent the majority of the day doing things that had been waiting to be done but were in the most obscure locations in the castle. I sorted through supplies in a room of the dungeon. I looked over the generators and examined some stone paths that had appeared recently at the back of the castle.

The sun had just begun to set as I headed out to find the bugs. I was feeling a lot better tonight. Distance was what I needed to get my emotions under control.

I'd avoided Cormac all day, in spite of the fact that he'd been looking for me, which made it all the sweeter. Every time I'd been greeted with, "Cormac was just here asking about you," the sun shone a little brighter in the sky.

I didn't worry about anyone being outside now. The night was the rippers' favorite time of day, which meant everyone else hated to leave the castle after dark. Even if you were immune to them, you never knew when they'd get hungry enough to lower their standards and you'd make it onto the menu. I personally hated lima beans, but that hadn't stopped me from choking some down tonight.

As I walked over the drawbridge, I noticed it had finally stopped snowing, but the low temperature still made your skin burn when a gust blew. I might not have noticed the note if it hadn't been so windy. It flapped against the only intact window of a burned out building that used to be a convenience store. The bright purple colored crayon writing caught my eye.

Go to Burrom's tree.

I knew exactly where they meant and I started walking. It was the tree in the golf course where Burrom had decided to go to rest. I looked behind me, waiting to see Cormac's hulking form as I trudged along through the snow. My toes already felt numb but I was pretty sure I had a higher than normal resistance to frostbite. Unfortunately, the snow wasn't blowing hard enough to cover my tracks and I wasn't special enough to magically make them disappear.

Or maybe I was.

"Come here, little ripper. No, that isn't right. Come here, freaky ripper, ripper, ripper." Hmmm, how did you go about calling these things? I'd never wanted to actively encourage their attention before. They just showed up.

I went through my entire cat and dog vernacular. Then I tried a clicking noise similar to their feeding sound. Nothing. These ugly fucks were the bane of my existence. Now, when I finally started to have uses for them, they seemed to be too busy to bother with me.

"Where are you?" I said out loud. Mist escaped out of my mouth as I spoke, which didn't freak me out anywhere close to how it used to, but instead of disappearing this time, it spiraled into the air and I heard my voice, but different, echoing on the air. "Where are you?" it repeated, over and over again.

Well, now, wasn't that an interesting parlor trick? That was way better than my smoke rings. Definitely going to use that at the next conference meeting.

And affective as well, as I saw the forms of the rippers appear in the distance a minute later.

And keep appearing.

"No, oh no. Not all of you!" Every ripper in the area was heading toward me. What was the point in having them cover my tracks if there were a hundred of them?

"Not all of you!" I tried to put a little umph into my words but there was no smoke, not even a wisp. I waved my hands back, but they didn't catch on and kept moving forward.

If this whacked out world could turn a casino into a castle and make bugs talk, was a user manual really that much to ask? I wished there were someone that could explain this particular magic, but of course the only other person that used it was my arch nemesis.

I rolled the term arch nemesis over my tongue a few more times. I kind of liked that title for the senator. Made me feel like a super hero.

"You three stay," I said to the first few who arrived. "You all," I waived my hands, trying to encompass everyone else, "Leave. Shoo."

Now, of course, because I was perpetually bungling this magic stuff up, they all started to leave, even the three I wanted. I threw my hands up. I was better off leaving tracks than walking around with a hoard of rippers, so I let them all leave.

It took me another half hour at a quick jog to get to Burrom's tree. It was easy to find, as it was the only one with bright green foliage in the middle of nothing but snow and ice.

As I approached the tree, I saw the bugs, but they weren't alone. A few jack rabbits sat near the base of the tree and a pair of owls were perched on a low lying branch. With each step, I prepared myself for the oddness I knew was about to come.

"Jo." The bugs greeted me first. "Our friends came. They wanted to meet you."

"Hi," I said awkwardly, not sure what to expect. I looked at the bunnies first and remembered the night I helped seal Burrom's hibernation ground. "Have we met before?"

They bobbed their little heads. "You hurt. We licked."

"Thank you," I said.

I looked at the owls next and they stared back, assessing me, angling their heads this way and that, deciding if I were prey. They made several humming noises as I waited for the verdict.

"Pretty, right?" the bugs said to the owls.

"Is she trustworthy, though?" the owls replied.

"We like her," the bunnies added, as they hopped over to my feet. I nearly jumped when I felt a little cold nose lift the hem of my pants and it pressed against the skin of my ankle. "I like her smell."

"Thank you."

"Put out your arms," one owl said.

I hesitated for a minute. Owls are a little scary up close, with their sharp beaks and talons. But if they were going to attack me, they probably would've done it already, so I decided to play along.

"To the sides, you silly girl," they said. "Not so bright," one owl told the other. I repositioned them to the sides in a scarecrow position and they both opened up their massive wings and landed on either arm. If that wasn't odd enough, they started to bounce up and down.

"What do you think?" the one on the left arm asked.

"Little springy, but it'll do. How is yours?"

"About the same. Let's swap."

A fluttering of wings had them switching places and proceeding with the bouncing again.

"Well?" the bugs asked. "What do you think?"

The owls bounced again for another moment before they flew back to their branch and announced their verdict. "She'll do. We will speak to her."

"Because you liked my arms?"

"We can't trust someone that has bad branches."

"What is it you want to trust me with?"

One of the bunnies stood on its hind legs. I was dying to scoop it up in my arms and pet it but I was afraid it might be insulted, so I tried to keep a business face on.

"The owls have seen things when they fly near the wall of wind. Strange gatherings are happening," the bunny explained.

"Yes," one owl spoke. "Bad things. The senator is forming an army."

This was the last thing I wanted to hear, but the very thing I expected. I was right. He was coming.

"How many did you see?" a deep familiar voice from behind me asked.

Shit. He'd followed me. I turned to see Cormac approach and then went back to do damage control. I needed this information and couldn't have all my feathered and fuzzy sources taking off.

The bugs were flying around in a frenzy, the bunnies were dashing behind a snow mound, but the owls remained calm and steady, holding the group loosely together with their confidence.

"Come forward, creature," the owls said to Cormac, which was a little bit pointless since he was moving toward them anyway.

"Hold out your arms."

Cormac looked to me and I nodded, and waved my hands upward, motioning for him to do it. I guess he missed the opening ceremonies.

Unlike me, he put them out to the sides first time and the owls flew over and each landed on an arm.

They started to bounce and then I heard the ooohs and aaahs start.

"Glorious branches," the one owl said.

"Yes, spectacular," the other agreed.

"Let's switch."

"Yes, yes!"

With a flapping of wings, they quickly exchanged places and the ooohing and ahhhing started up again. The bunnies, which were peeking out from behind the snow mounds, approached Cormac. They seemed more confident after the owls' approval and started to sniff around his ankles.

"Hmmm, it smells good," one bunny said, at the same time an owl looked to be nuzzling at Cormac's neck.

The only thing that stopped me from losing my mind at this love fest was the bugs, who swarmed next to me, clearly not as willing to join Cormac's fan club. I took a couple of steps closer to the owls and Cormac.

"I hate to interrupt anything, but could we get back to the business of armies?"

I was taken aback by Cormac's laughter.

"Nothing about this is funny," I said as I gave him the nastiest look I could drum up, which by the way, was pretty damn mean.

"They're tickling me," he said and laughed again. "Stop."

I looked at the owl nuzzling him and just rolled my eyes.

"Come on, she's right." He lifted his arms in an encouraging manner. "Time to go back to your branches."

One of the bugs flew and landed on the tip of my ear and whispered, "Don't worry, Jo, we don't like him either."

I had a feeling Cormac heard, since the smile fell from his face and he became all business again as both the owls returned to their real branch.

"Do you know how many?" I asked.

"Many and many," the owls responded in a grave tone.

"Many like a thousand? Or more like ten thousand?"

When the owls looked the other way without replying, one of the bugs spoke. "The owls can't count."

"Yes, we can."

"Then how many?" the bugs chimed back.

"Lots, too many to count."

Which meant the bugs were probably correct. The owls couldn't count. It could be ten, ten thousand or just a few hundred, for all we knew, and shed very little light on the threat posed.

"What did they look like? Did they look human?" Cormac asked.

"Strange creatures. Humans, too. But mostly strange."

I'd thought I was going to have more time to prepare. One would think after you learned you might live forever, barring a nasty accident or murder, that time wouldn't be as much of an obstacle. Unfortunately, life around you didn't stagnate in respect for new longevity.

We took turns pressing the owls for more details but all we got was more of the same. Lots of "strange creatures," which I assumed were the *changed* and "many."

Cormac and I thanked them with an agreement that they'd inform us of anything else they saw and headed back toward the castle.

We were about halfway back and my mind was racing with possibilities when Cormac spoke. "You should've been preparing this entire time."

My jaw dropped open at the audacity of the

statement. "Don't tell me what I should've been doing after you dropped the ball. I've had my hands full just trying to keep everyone fed and intact. You've got a lot of nerve, casting any judgments."

I ran in front of him, stopping him and ready to lay into him more, when I saw the smile on his face.

"Why are you smiling?"

"Because you just made the point for me. You did the best you could in a bad situation. This isn't your fault."

"I can't let the senator take what little they have left." I turned away from him and started walking again. I didn't want him to see how close to breaking down I was.

"We won't."

I shook my head. "Cormac, there is no more 'we'."

He didn't say anything and I didn't look at him as we fell back into silence.

***

I stared at the small group gathered in the penthouse. It was only the people who were absolutely trustworthy. There were the old standbys, Buzz, Dodd, Dark and Burrom, and the new kids, Colleen, Sharon, Chip and Katie.

"I'm sorry I called you all here without notice but we've got some intel. It's not good." I'd sent Dark, the first person I saw upon our arrival back, to round them up while I changed into clothes that weren't soaked through with melted snow. In true Dark efficiency, he had everyone there by time I'd pulled on dry jeans and a sweater.

"What's up?" Dark asked, speaking for everyone.

"Looks like the senator is preparing to move against us." I looked over at Cormac, who stood there expressionless, waiting to see if he was going to contribute. I looked around the room as everyone still had their eyes trained on me. "There is news that he's gathering together an army."

"Who's the source? Is it reliable?" Colleen asked.

"I trust it. I don't have any more details right now. But I don't know when, or how many. That's what we need to find out." I perched on the arm of one sofa, swinging my leg. "I'm going to ask the senator for a meeting on his turf."

The immediate roar of "no's" that came from the group surprised me. I was expecting push back from Cormac, but not the emphatic response from everyone else.

Dark grabbed my arm from where he sat next to me on the couch. "If you die, we might all be screwed."

It wasn't the exact sentiment you want to hear at the thought of your death but I understood enough to joke about it. "Please, Dark, I know you care for me and all but hold yourself together, man."

The ramifications of my death weren't something any of us ever openly discussed. No one was sure if the theory that my death could possibly kill everyone was correct or not.

"For the same reason you don't want me to go, I'm the perfect distraction. He won't kill me. And while I'm there, drawing his attention, you can get in easier and see what we're up against." Their expressions looked hesitant and I waited for someone to argue the point but it was Cormac who finally decided to speak.

"No." It was a single command, not up for debate.

"The way things are run have changed since you left. We're a democracy now." I turned to look at him. He was standing with a hand resting above the fireplace, his body angled away from it, and the firelight made his eyes nearly glow. I broke eye contact first, his full attention unsettling me in ways I'd prefer not to acknowledge.

No one else in the room seemed to have a problem staring at the two of us. I actually thought that perhaps I should move closer to him so they didn't have to strain their necks back and forth between the two of us.

"This is my building, my call," he said from across the room.

"And it's my body." Why didn't I say my

choice? I didn't need to look at him to know he'd picked up on the slip. He caught everything.

"This is a business matter. I thought we were in agreement?" I said.

"We didn't agree on this."

No one spoke as we played verbal ping-pong.

"I've been around a lot longer than you. My word is still final in this place."

"Not anymore. You've been gone and things changed."

The words were out before I even thought about the fact that I'd just thrown down the gauntlet and in front of witnesses. I was pinning him into a corner and neither of us would back down from the fight.

It didn't matter. I'd said it and I'd meant it. I wasn't looking to fight with him, but I wasn't living under anyone's rule, not even Cormac's.

I waited for the response that surely would come but the only thing he did was eye up the rest of the room. En mass, they grabbed their stuff and quickly left at the silent order. It was hard not to be envious of the silent command. Last time I'd tried that, people asked if I had something stuck in my eye. Maybe I squinted too much.

No time to ponder it now as WWVI, or whatever number we were up to—seriously, who could keep track, anymore—was about to go down.

As the last footsteps faded away and I knew we

were the only ones left in the room, I turned, prepared for battle.

And he was smiling?

"What's wrong with you?" This was worse than a fight. Maybe he was all messed up from the magic. I didn't like when he smiled; he had dimples to die for. I really needed to stay grounded, but it's odd how dents in someone's face could add so much appeal.

"Nothing." Still smiling, God damn his dimpled face.

"Why did you send everyone out?"

"Because I can't let them think I'm fine with what you just did. They'd think I went soft. Next thing you know, people would stop listening to my orders and then I'd have to kill someone. This seemed easier. Let them think I'm beating you in private." He flashed me a smile in contrast to his statement.

"Well, just stop looking at me like that."

"Like what?" He moved a few feet closer and leaned a hip against the bar, smirking now.

"Like you're proud of me or something."

He crossed his arms over his chest, perfectly relaxed while I felt ready to jump out of my skin. And it all came down to time, again. He'd had plenty of it and I'd swear it gave him an edge in dealing with emotions. Then I saw his chest rise a little bit more rapidly than it should for someone completely relaxed. I realized the only thing time had done was let him fake it better.

"What's wrong with that?"

"Everything. You don't get to be proud of me, or look at me like that. I'm not your daughter, wife or friend. We are business associates. That's it." I stood and stepped a few feet closer, making a waving gesture to encompass my body. "You have no ownership of this that should inspire pride within your being."

"And yet, I have this strange warm fuzziness inside that feels oddly like pride. Strange." He made a mocking show of surprise.

"Just stop."

"If you don't like how I look at you, ignore me."

I turned and walked to the table and decided to do exactly that. I put my head down and looked at the schedules I needed to get done and tried to pretend he wasn't even in the room. We had to kill at least another thirty minutes alone to keep up the charade, one I was willing to go along with if it kept the peace.

He came over and leaned a hip on the table right beside me. "Unless, that is, you can't?"

"I can ignore you just fine." I flipped a page over. "See this? I'm ignoring you right this very second."

He moved closer, leaning over me. "Really?"

His fingers trailed over my arm.

"Yes." I refused to look at him again to confirm just how well I was ignoring him.

As his hand pushed my hair away from my neck, I was determinedly not going to turn into his arms. He'd left and I had some pride. I wasn't going to just fall at his feet now that he decided to return.

Then his lips made contact with my skin.

"I'm trying to work."

"Don't let me stop you."

"You're in my way." I motioned to how he was obscuring my papers, as if that was the only issue I had with this situation, not that my own chest was rising with my ragged breaths.

"Sorry, I'll get out of your way."

Instead of leaving though, he just stepped behind me, one arm wrapped around my waist as his other cupped my breast and his lips returned to my neck.

It was too much. I sighed and leaned back into him with a groan, thinking maybe, just this once. How bad could that really be? One time. What was one time?

And then he spoke and ruined it.

"You might have forgotten you're mine, but your body hasn't."

I pushed out of his embrace. "This isn't a game to me."

"You think I enjoy this?" His voice was low,

soft and intense. *Now,* he was mad. "I came back, thinking about seeing you, only you. And what do I get? You basically tell me to go fuck myself. Nice homecoming."

"What did you expect, when you leave me with barely a goodbye? Just leave with no warning?"

He didn't answer but stormed into the bedroom and slammed the door.

"Hey! Now who's running?" I yelled. I wasn't sure if going into the bedroom was technically 'running' but he wasn't arguing. I wasn't above taking a point on default. If this *was* a game, at least I was winning.

Until I looked at the couch, also my bed for the night. Okay, maybe more like tied. It was hard to sell a win when you were walking bent over from a cramp in your back.

Chapter Eleven

Letting Loose

After last night, I was relieved at the prospect of unleashing some energy. With nowhere else to train, Burrom and I had cleared out the conference room for the time being and laid out whatever exercise mats we could find, padding yoga mats up in the gaps left. It looked a little ragtag so it was a good thing I healed quickly.

"I still don't see the point of this. I need to be working on controlling the magic, not wasting time." My hands were planted firmly on my yoga pant clad hips.

"I would've agreed with you until a few months ago. A pair of handcuffs, a piece of duct tape and you were useless." He tilted his head toward me, daring me to deny it.

"Okay, I see your point." There was no use in denying that before Burrom had shown up and a swarm of bugs flew to my rescue, I'd been cooked. "But I want it down, for the record, that I let them do that to me."

"If I were keeping a record, for your sake, I wouldn't write that down." He made a sour face in mocking.

"Whatever, tough guy. Let's get this going." I

slipped off my sneakers and stepped onto the mat, ready to kick some butt.

"I don't want you to use any of your Keeper tricks."

Or get my butt kicked. My fun afternoon just took nosedive. "Why not?"

"Because you don't know if they'll always work. What if he has some Keepers in his pocket, like Tracker did? What then? It's not like he hasn't been in cahoots with them before."

"Fine." I redid my ponytail and motioned for him to come at me. "No Keeper tricks. And, just for the record you won't keep, no one says cahoots anymore."

Now, for any of you that think when you see a 200 lb plus man heading toward you, even in sparring, you don't get at least slightly anxious, you're either crazy or you have bigger balls than I do.

So when Burrom came at me, I didn't mean to zap him with my Keeper tricks, or bring him to his knees gasping, it just happened.

I cringed as I watched him, palm on the mat, trying to catch his breath.

"I'm so sorry, Burrom." I leaned down slightly and moved my hand in the direction of his shoulder but froze. He might not want me to touch him right now.

"I thought we agreed you wouldn't do that." His

breathing evened out but his tone was of someone still in pain.

"I didn't do it on purpose." I folded my hands together in front of me to avoid the urge to touch him.

He stood up slowly, looking like he was trying to shake off the pain in his arm, where I'd made contact.

He walked to the other side of the room and then turned and waited for me to look ready. But when I nodded I was, he shook his head and walked off a couple of steps.

"This isn't going to work."

"Why? I promise I'm not going to zap you again." I held both palms up.

"And you are going to do it anyway. If you did it before, when you were more relaxed, you're definitely going to do it now when you look like that."

"Like what?"

"All on edge."

"Well, stop scowling at me then."

"I'm sorry. It's hard not to scowl when my arm is still throbbing." He didn't sound sorry. He sounded like he wanted to throttle me.

I watched as he went and grabbed his funny phone from where it had been tucked in his shoe in the corner.

"Who you calling?" I had a bad feeling about

this.

He held up his finger. "Can you meet me in the conference room for a little sparring?"

He said thanks and hung up before I could stop him.

"That better have been Dodd."

"Dodd isn't as good."

"Tell me you didn't just call Cormac?"

"I had to."

"And he's coming?"

He nodded.

It was my turn to pace away from him in annoyance. "I want to kill you right now."

"This is business. You go down and I'm sinking right along with you."

"Dodd would have been fine and you know it." I crossed my arms in front of my chest as I narrowed my eyes.

"Dodd would've pulled his punches."

"Oh, well yeah, that would've sucked." I snorted in annoyance and waited for Cormac to show.

I was sitting against the wall, kicking at the mat when he filled the doorway. I didn't look directly at him and he returned the favor.

"How's it going?" he asked Burrom.

"I tried. I can't do it."

"I didn't think it was going to work."

"You said this was your idea?" I accused

Burrom.

"Technically, it was mine, Cormac just mentioned the need for it and he made really valid points."

Cormac looked around the room. "I can't spar here. It's too small. Let's go outside."

That got me to my feet and ended the charade of nonchalance. "It's cold, about to get dark, and worse, people will be able to see us." Did I have to explain this all to him?

"And you think you're always going to get to choose where you fight? It might be cold, dark and have people then, too."

"Fine," I was on a real winning streak now. "Let me get my jacket."

"No. The last thing you want is a bunch of bulky clothes when you fight. And if you know you're about to be attacked, get rid of them."

If it had been anyone else bossing me around right now, I swear, it would've been so much easier to be mature. But it wasn't.

It was Cormac. And I wasn't in a good enough mental place to deal with this, but I would. I wasn't ready to have this much psychical contact either, but again, I would. Why? Because I *was* in the mood to beat the hell out of him. And if I had to stay out there all day and night, I was determined to get a couple of good shots in. So when he turned and started walking, I followed after, a respectable distance away and enough space between us to interrogate Burrom.

"Can't believe you sold me out." I punched his arm as he walked next to me, Cormac in view ahead.

"Me? I had to apologize for like three hours just for getting in bed with you. I *have* to play nice now."

"Really?"

"Yes. It was exhausting. He even threatened to pull the liquor license on my club."

"Uh, there are no more liquor licenses."

"Not according to Cormac."

A twinge of guilt replaced the annoyance I'd been feeling. "I really didn't mean to give you up like that."

"Just get a good shot in for me."

It was still light out when we stepped into the courtyard, but I was grateful no one was paying much attention to us. I had no delusions, though. The small amount of privacy probably wouldn't last long.

Cormac stopped as he reached the center of the courtyard, about ten feet away from me.

"Give me everything you've got," he said. "Don't hold back."

"Nothing to worry about there," I countered, staring at him across from me in a snug shirt and work out pants.

"You know, all you are doing is misdirecting energy."

"You're saying my anger is misdirected..." I left the word *desire* off the sentence because there were some people listening.

"That's exactly what I'm saying."

"Absolutely not. Right now, I don't even like you."

He tilted his head back as he laughed. "Not only do you like me, but you might even?" He left the word love off and smiled mockingly.

"I do not."

"And even though you seem to have a violent streak," he paused taking in my lethal stare, "that might be getting worse, I'm still willing to have you."

"Just shut up and start."

"When you do fight, you can be an attacker, or counter fighter. Your short stature is going to be a problem, since you'll have to overcome your opponent's reach. In your case, I think you would be better off waiting for them to approach you and then try and catch an opening."

"Do something, already."

I held up my hands, trying to protect my face and ribs as I waited for him. I didn't have any formal training but I had gone through Oslo's street fighting boot camp. That's what we used to jokingly call it. I knew every dirty trick there was and had no shame using them.

We circled each other, as I eyed up potential weaknesses. Problem was, I didn't think he had any. I knew that I, on the other hand, had a ton. I probably weighed less than half of him, and couldn't move anywhere near as fast.

He lunged for me. I knew he was only moving at half speed because I dodged him easily. He made another halfhearted attempt. I've seen him move, he could be a hell of a lot quicker than that. Quick enough, in fact, that I wouldn't even see him if he didn't want me to.

"Now this is just getting insulting." I dropped my guard and stood still. "If we are going to do this, let's do it."

He didn't say anything but he nodded. His next move, all I saw was a blur and then I was catching my breath while lying flat on my back. Cormac's hand hovered over me, offering me help up. I ignored it and got to my feet unaided. I brushed off the residual snow from my back. The snow had been shoveled from the front courtyard but a thin coating remained.

I'd asked for this but it was still frustrating when I wanted to be the one kicking some butt. I prepared myself and looked around. A handful of people had made their way outside and were standing back watching and whispering. Here came the audience.

He'd left me and now thought he was going to publicly kick my ass? I didn't think so.

We began to circle each other again. This time I was going to really concentrate, block out everything but him.

"Try to use your legs. Your upper body can't compete with me, but your legs might."

I didn't speak or tell him to shut up and fight. I was going to remain calm and concentrated. No more blurry man moves taking me by surprise.

And then I was on my back. Again. I sucked wind for a minute, waiting for the air to inflate my lungs back up. If I didn't know how quickly I'd heal, I might be a bit concerned over the ache I was already feeling. This time, he didn't bother offering me his hand. I got to my feet again, although a bit slower.

I didn't bother wiping the snow off, considering I might be back in it in another second. When I turned to get a lock on Cormac's position, I cringed. We'd gained an even greater audience.

I'd worked hard to keep control of this place when he'd left. I'd earned respect. Even the ones that didn't like me, and there were a lot, still gave me my due. I wasn't going to get my ass kicked in front of everyone. I needed to change tactics. Waiting for the blows to come and counter attacking wasn't working. I needed to go on the offensive.

"You ready?" he asked.

I nodded but before he had the chance to attack, I moved in as quickly as I could push myself. And I caught big fat air. He dodged my swing as if I were a child fighting Goliath.

"Time!" Burrom called from the side. "Need to speak to my fighter."

"Time? What?" Cormac yelled back.

"I said time!"

"This isn't a boxing match."

Burrom ignored him and yelled for someone to get him a stool. I walked over to him where he stood surrounded by the ever increasing crowd. A stool was plunked down in front of me and I gratefully sat.

He handed me a water bottle right before he laid into me. "What are you doing out there?"

"Getting my ass kicked?"

I looked over to where Cormac waited, now with Dodd and Dark. Traitors.

"You are magic."

I shook my head. "He is, too. And right now, I'm closer to pummeled raw meat."

"He might have some magic, but you've got more. Start channeling it. You're so in your head that you aren't letting it flow. You're lost before you even swing. Stop being the old Jo and be the woman I've seen you become in the last three months. Stop thinking. Trust me, it's doing you absolutely no good."

As far as pep talks, I'd heard better; *given* better, I think. But I'd give it a try. I nodded, and stood up. When I walked back into the clearing, now lined with people, I knew this was it. I was either going to show him, and the crowd, I was someone to be reckoned with, or I'd lose all the respect I'd built.

I took a long slow breath and focused on letting it all go, the panic, the preconceptions of failure, not being good enough, everything. I reached out around me to every ounce of magic I could. Anybody looking might mistake it as my frozen breath on the air but I felt it flowing to me. I was trying to absorb it and channel it. And I could feel it working.

Cormac stood ten feet away, waiting. I nodded I was ready and then so did he. The second his head moved, I let the magic burst through me. I didn't know what it would do, what I could do. I was just acting and reacting.

I was operating on sheer instinct and I was fucking amazing. I leapt into the air a split second before I reached Cormac, did a twist to evade his hands and planted my foot on his chest. I sent him sprawling as I landed softly and untouched behind him.

I whipped around as he was getting to his feet, surprise on his face, and I thought maybe a hint of pride?

"I told you about that look," I halfheartedly warned him.

"I'm sure I have no idea what you are talking about." He was smiling as he said it. He was impressed.

"You ready to go again?" It felt good to be the one standing, waiting for him to signal he'd recouped enough to continue.

I was bouncing from foot to foot, pulling as much energy as I could to me, feeling almost high from it.

"You under control?" Cormac asked, his stare turning from impressed to slightly suspicious.

"You trying to stall?"

He waved his hand in a bring-it-on motion. This little demonstration had just taken on a new life. A look around showed even more people, perhaps half the castle, stood watching, hanging on our every movement. They stood as close as they could without risking direct participation.

And were they betting? I'll be damned if I didn't hear wagers being called out.

I turned back to Cormac and it was clear this practice had just turned serious for him. Where he was soft pedaling before, I could see the changes in him, and he looked like he was happy about it. I realized he was excited for a real challenge. It made sense. He probably didn't get one often and I was feeling pumped up that I was the one bringing it to him.

I didn't think about what I was going to do. I just trusted my body and the magic streaming through me to handle the details.

We circled each other like two well-paired combatants. When he came for me again, instead of the blur he'd been before, I could see him with perfect clarity. The overload of magic pumping through me was heightening my senses. As he neared, I jumped into the air and did a back flip, landing easily out of reach.

He turned to my new position. His face full of questions. A single silent question on his lips. *How?*

I smiled in response, offering no insight, as I pulled as much magic to me as I possibly could. And that's when I looked around and realized it was everywhere.

I'd felt the magic for a while, but I was actually seeing it, waves in different colors, layering through the air. I lifted my hand right where a swell of purple mist was and pulled at it. I could see my body absorbing it as it flowed right into my hand.

"Jo?" Cormac asked as I seemed to drift off into my own world.

"I'm ready," I said as I gave him back my full attention.

I moved a couple of steps to my left as he moved with me, both of us looking for an opening. Suddenly, in a burst of movement, even quicker than the first time he came at me, he attacked with a swift kick designed to take my legs out. But I jumped into the air, flipped over him and caught him with a sidekick to the back rib area.

I was on fire.

And suddenly, I wasn't feeling so hot.

He spun around, seemingly undaunted by a kick I knew would've cracked a lesser man's ribs. He was hopping from foot to foot now looking invigorated. The guy could take a beating with style.

Then the expression on his face changed. He dropped his fighter stance and walked toward me.

"Jo? You okay?" He stood only inches away from me.

"I'm not sure," I said in an equally hushed voice. I looked at him, asking without words to end this somehow without alerting everyone watching that was something was amiss as my gaze scanned the crowd

He did a single nod. "You might not like how I achieve your exit."

He closed the last of the distance between us, one arm circled my back while the other moved to the back of my head.

I made it easy for him as my mouth gaped open, surprised with the way he'd decided to accomplish his goal. His lips covered mine softly, and I felt his tongue trace my own. "You didn't think it would be free, did you?" his lips whispered, still so close.

He leaned his head back, but kept an arm around me as I was snug to him. "Fight's over!" he yelled to the crowd.

He leaned back down and whispered in my ear, "Can you walk?"

"Not sure."

I was trying to keep up appearances but my hands were shaking, my gaze on him.

He swept me up in his arms, leaning down and kissing me before he started to walk.

"Get a room," I heard Burrom yell in the background as we left.

Chapter Twelve

We've All Got Our Kryptonite

"Jo!"

I woke up to Cormac repeating my name. I was laid out on the couch in the penthouse. Oh no, I must have actually passed out on the way up here.

"I'm awake. There's no reason to keep shaking so vigorously," I said as Cormac's hands gripped my shoulders.

"How do you feel?" He stopped the movement but his hands remained in a tight grip on my shoulders.

"Like I drank too much." I pushed myself up and he finally loosened his hold. I looked around, expecting to find more eyes on me but it was only Cormac and Burrom in the room.

Cormac turned on Burrom. "What the hell did you do to her?"

"I didn't do this! And you better watch who you're talking to like that, because I'm the one that had her back when you disappeared."

"Yeah, I heard about that. And just so you know, I don't care what the hell you are, you start to lose your usefulness and I'll take you out. Watch your step."

"Just try it."

The two of them had an odd relationship. I didn't know quite how long they'd known each other, but I was guessing it was decades. I knew they wouldn't actually hurt each other. And even though I didn't think either one would ever admit it, they liked each other. It wasn't a bromance exactly, but more of a "deep down you're not so bad and I won't kill you kind of way."

"Guys, when you're done bickering with each other, I think I might have an idea what actually happened."

They both whipped around back to me. "What?" they said in unison.

"I could see it." I was amazed myself thinking back. I'd felt almost high at the time and I didn't think I could truly describe the beauty or the heady feeling I'd gotten from it.

"See what?" Cormac asked.

"The magic." I looked at Burrom. "You know how you thought I was a sort of vessel or divining rod for the magic? When we closed the holes, especially the one in New York, I pulled energy from the other Keepers. Well, when I was fighting tonight, I tried to pull it to me from the atmosphere and it worked."

Feeling better, the excitement of what had just happened poured through me. I stood, and paced the room unable to sit still. They both watched me as the pieces fell into place in my mind. "It was crazy.

After a certain point, I could see it. The magic, I could actually see its brilliant colors, swirling in the air. I could watch it enter my body."

"But what happened? Why did you collapse?" Cormac asked. He grabbed a napkin from the bar area. Walking over to where I was walking in circles. "Hold still."

"What?"

He tilted my head and pressed the napkin near my ear. When he pulled it back, there was blood on it and he looked like he wanted to punch Burrom again.

"A couple drops of blood aren't a big deal." I grabbed the bloodied napkin and tossed it in the trash. "I just overloaded. I didn't know there was a limit to how much I could pull in. I'll go lighter next time."

"Maybe you just need to get used to it?" Burrom asked, focusing more on the potential as I was than the ramifications.

"Or maybe it will kill her next time." Cormac shoved Burrom on the shoulder. It wasn't hard enough to push him over, but a warning none the less.

"But it might not." Burrom moved a hand to shove Cormac back but then paused it mid air before dropping it, leaving Cormac untouched.

"You've got more blood coming from your ears," Cormac said.

I reached my hand up and lowered it to find my fingers were red.

"Don't you get it? You're still bleeding. This isn't something to play around with." His fingers cupped my chin as his eyes roved over my face.

I pulled away from him and the concern I saw. "But who knows what I could do? The senator is coming. We can't leave anything on the table." I walked as far as I could away from Cormac before I uttered my next words. "I sent him a message, telling him I want a meeting. He's expecting me in five days."

"To the senator? When did you do that?" I knew what Cormac was really thinking though. How did I get it past his spies?

"Right after I told everyone I wanted a meeting."

"I can't believe you did that. What about the 'this is a democracy' speech? I guess that only pertained to me?"

I'd known he was going to be pissed but he'd get over it. What choice did he have? I hadn't left him with any.

"Who'd you send?"

"It doesn't matter," I said, evading the question.

He turned to a too-quiet Burrom. "You delivered it."

"I thought it was a sound idea."

"Yes, because you don't give a shit if she dies."

"No, I'm just a pragmatist. Of course I care if she dies. It might be my ass on the line with her."

Cormac stared at him with such anger I wasn't surprised when Burrom made an excuse of wanting to stay out of our fight and left the penthouse.

"I'm going with you," Cormac said.

"I don't think that's a good idea."

"Why?"

"It's just a hunch, but the entire time you were gone, there seemed to be a certain amiable peace between me and the senator. I think this recent turmoil has something to do with you coming back."

"Then he won't know I'm there. You aren't going in alone."

I knew I wasn't going to be able to deter and I didn't want to. This is what I'd been angling for the entire time.

"Fine. We'll get a group together. You handle the intel and I'll be the distraction."

Chapter Thirteen

Awkward Exits

"I don't like this." Cormac punched the stone of the wall as he paced the room. He'd been periodically punching things all day and I'd been graciously not commenting on it.

"I've got to go." I ducked just as a chip of stone came flying my way.

He didn't say anything else but he was pacing. I hated when he paced. It made me nervous, surprisingly more than the punching of random items.

He paused and crossed his arms, and just when I thought he was going to start in with a new tirade of why I shouldn't, he surprised me and said, "I know."

That was easier than I'd expected. I looked back down at the maps on the table I was studying. Unfortunately, just because a monster was preparing for war on us, it didn't mean we could stop daily functions. Well, technically we could stop but we'd also not eat and that wasn't getting a lot of votes.

But it was really hard to focus with everything going on and Cormac pacing around like a powder keg with a lit fuse. Every one of my senses was attuned to him. I knew the instant his path changed from where he'd been wearing holes in the floor to across the room where I was standing at the table I liked to use as my desk.

I tried my darnedest to ignore him, but when his features softened from frustration to a new emotion, it was pretty difficult.

"I warned you about those looks," I said as I could see the pride in his eyes.

"How long do you plan on sleeping on the couch?"

He took a step closer and picked up a lock of my hair in his hands, splaying it in his fingers and then running it down the length of my arm. I'd wished I'd thrown on a sweatshirt instead of the tank top but the fireplace didn't come with a thermostat and I'd added too many logs again.

I wanted to pull back but that would mean he was affecting me. He was, but I could pretend.

"Depends. How long do you plan on occupying the bed while you pretend to sleep? And could you fake snore a little more quietly?"

His deep laughter filled the penthouse and the masculine sound sent a shiver through me.

He leaned a hip on the table as he perused me.

It was getting harder to fake nonchalance when I saw the look in his eyes change from pride to something a lot hotter. His stare was so intense that if he kept it up, I didn't think he'd have to do much more than that and I'd be hopping into bed with him. As it was, every day that passed I started to forget why I was even mad.

"I'm really impressed with the way you stepped up."

"Thank you." I instantly thought of the rules I'd made up in my head for Cormac management. Don't smile. You do not need his approval. Do not encourage speaking when he is looking at you like that. There were other rules, but I couldn't seem to remember them anymore.

"How long do you think it's going to take for you to get past being angry at me for leaving?"

"I'm not angry." Don't engage. Don't admit to anger.

His left hand moved deeper into my hair and started to massage the back of my head. Then it moved down to my neck to do the same. Contact made. We were about to hit def con five.

"Liar," he said teasingly.

Resist the dimples. Do not look at the dimples. They are defects. Shit, must ignore the dents.

"Think what you want." I was trying to keep myself so concentrated on the maps in front of me I didn't see his next move coming until I was pulled in between his legs.

"I need to work," I said, turning my head to the side, not thinking of the clear opening I was providing until I felt his lips skimming along my collar bone, working a slow path across.

"Then work," he whispered, his hands roving along my back, massaging all the strength from my body. "Go ahead." His mouth moved up to my jaw line as I realized his grip was anything but tight. I could have easily removed myself from his embrace.

"*Sure*. Until I try to move." Did either of us believe what I'd just said? His hands were barely a feather on me now, gliding up and down my arms and then down my back, feather light over my hips.

Both his hands moved into my hair as he turned my face to meet his. "Pretend whatever you want." The words feathered against my lips just before he kissed me.

Three long months without this and getting a taste of him brought it all back. I knew contact was going to be my undoing. I wrapped my arms tightly around him, pulling him closer, and a tsunami of need unleashed between us.

An arm wrapped around my waist as his other hand pulled my leg up to wrap around him. My hands gripped his hair, bringing his mouth to mine.

My head fell back as his hand grabbed my ass and fitted me perfectly to him.

Then the door slammed shut.

"Shit. I didn't lock the door."

"Whoa, sorry," Dark said as he stepped in the doorway to the living room before we'd even separated.

I jumped back quickly, putting a healthy distance between him and me.

"No, it's fine. What's up?" I said, looking anywhere but at Cormac, who was looking only at me.

"Just wanted to know if you worked out the scouting schedules yet?"

"Yeah, I've got most of it done. It's on the table," I said, pointing to where Cormac still leaned. "You can let everyone know what the schedule is. I've got to go make a run and talk to Colleen. See you guys later." I would've run from the room if I thought I could've pulled it off without looking ridiculous. As it was, I was bordering on awkward with my fast walk.

I didn't breathe right until I hit the stairwell and there were no footsteps behind me. I flew down the stairs, trying to put as much space between Cormac and me as I could.

"Jo?" I didn't recognize the voice coming from behind me but I did remember the face when I turned. He wasn't overly handsome, with a very plain shade of brown hair but with enough scars running across his face to make him memorable. It was one of the wolves I didn't have much interaction with. He used to hang around with Rogo a lot, before he lost his head.

I stopped to talk to him, not alarmed at all

being alone with one wolf in the stairwell. I could take him down easily.

"Yes?" I asked as I waited for him to speak.

"I've been wanting to talk to you." I could hear the nervousness in his voice but that wasn't surprising. There were three categories of people these days. The ones that hated me but were still respectful, because they didn't want to get booted. The ones that feared me because nobody was really sure exactly what I was, and the ones that liked me. They were mostly *changed* and made up the smallest percentage.

"What's up?"

"I'd like to get in on some of the scouting rounds."

Every creature immune to rippers wanted to be on scouting duty now. It was a license to steal. I didn't know what percentage I lost off the top but I'd accepted it as an unavoidable expense. I only had so many honest people and it was either take the loss or work the few good ones into the ground.

"I'll think about it. Give Dark your name and room number when you see him. I'll figure out if we can use you on a run when I do the next schedule."

I went to turn, considering our conversation over when he grabbed my arm.

I looked down at the hand gripping my forearm and back to his face, sending a silent warning with my expression. He smartly snatched his hand back and quickly spoke in explanation. "I just had a couple of more questions."

Maybe it was my annoyance at this wolf, or maybe it was my emotional turmoil about Cormac, but I didn't hear anyone come up behind me. I wasn't aware of the danger looming until I felt the pinch of the needle that sealed my fate.

***

When I came to, my mouth was gagged, my legs were tied and my hands were bound behind my back. A strip of fabric blocked my vision. If that wasn't bad enough, I was cramped in what felt like a box. I couldn't stretch out my legs, and my knees were pressed against my chest as I lay on my side. The box swayed up and down with the carrier's steps. The slightest draft of air came through a crack, or maybe a hole they'd drilled. It was alarming and comforting at the same time. I wouldn't die from suffocation, but I might be in here a while.

I could hear people, a lot of them. I didn't know how much time had passed, but maybe we hadn't left the casino yet.

I tried to scream past the gag but it didn't work. So I started to roll from side to side in the little room I had and bang against the box as much as I could.

"Go in there for a minute," I could hear a man's muffled voice say.

I felt the air as soon as the cover was lifted and a pinch immediately followed.

"I told you it wasn't enough. She could've totally screwed us." My head felt fuzzy and nausea threatened. I tried to breathe deeply through my nose. With a gag, throwing up could be deadly. Everything went black.

When I woke again, some unknown time later, shivering, my blindfold had loosened just enough that I could see partially out of one eye. It would've been pitch black except for the fire burning outside where I lay, in a nylon tent. I saw glimpses of the flames whenever the flap of the entrance opened with a strong gust of wind. A full moon highlighted the snow around the shadow of four huddled bodies.

I didn't need to test the binds on my ankles or wrists to know how tight they were. The rope burned where it dug into my flesh. I tried to pull magic, but whatever they had shot me up with clung like a lead balloon to my consciousness, making it a fight to even remain awake. No matter how hard I tried, I couldn't muster up even a wisp.

"Are you sure this was the best way?" I heard one of them say. It sounded like the wolf that had stopped me in the hallway.

I just wanted to lie there in the drug-induced oblivion, but I had to concentrate.

"It was only a matter of time before she figured out who we are," another one said.

Who they were? I knew it was the wolves.

"How? We could have stayed there forever. She might not ever have known," the first wolf replied.

"If she didn't figure it out, the senator would've told her. We're better off with him, anyway. When he attacks, you know he's going to win. The freaks he's got over there? It's going to be a bloodbath. No, delivering her to the senator in exchange for protection was the right thing to do."

"Maybe that was a bluff to get us to do this?" One of the other two finally spoke. "Other than us, there's no one left that was there that night."

"It doesn't matter," the final silhouette said. "Either way we'd be sitting ducks. She would've figured it out. She's weird. She knew I was watching her even though there was absolutely no way she should've. Who knows what shit she can do."

"Yeah, he's right. Once she knew we were the ones that killed her mother, there'd be no turning back."

Even dazed as I was, the anger roiled off me, cutting through the haze that clung to my mind.

"Shit!" A flap opened and I could see the mist starting to gather around me, signaling the magic starting to gather.

"Get the needle, quick!" They scrambled as I focused on the anger I felt, using the adrenaline to help clear my thoughts. These were the people that robbed me of a mother. Now they were packaging me up and handing me over to the senator?

But before I could do anything, the pinch of the needle and the heaviness of the drugs seized my revenge from me.

"Did you smell the anger coming off of her?"

Shit, I thought as I faded. That's how they'd known I was coming around. They'd smelled it. Where was a ripper when you needed one?

"Give her another, just in case."

I felt another pinch and wondered if I'd ever wake up.

***

I heard shuffling noises near my head.

"If we keep drugging her, we might kill her."

Rough hands turned me on my side.

"We're only doing what the senator asked."

"But what about the rumor? You know…the *rumor.*"

"We're dead either way, if we don't get her to him. Does it matter how we go?"

More feet moved near my head. I felt a tug on my scalp as a foot stepped on my hair.

"And we can't get past the check points. We don't have a choice."

I wanted to open my eyes but I couldn't get them to lift. I couldn't get anything to move, my limbs felt like they weighed a hundred pounds each and my tongue was swollen in my mouth from dehydration. The nausea roiled through me from the drugs and I started violently dry heaving before they stole my consciousness again.

Crazy drug induced nightmares filled my mind with screaming, crying and blood spraying everywhere. Limbs flew, leaving puddles of red in their wake. I dreamt of the rippers and they were making screeching noises that pierced my eardrums; then everything went silent.

I awoke to pain ripping across my face. I thought it was going to be them, the wolves who'd abducted me, but it was Cormac, a piece of duct tape in his hand.

I tried to speak but my mouth was painfully dry and he held a water bottle to my lips for a moment before he reached behind me to cut the binds. I squinted past the light and tried to focus clearly beyond a few feet in front of me.

"What..." I didn't know what to say as I looked around. There was blood everywhere, like in my nightmare. Bodies, or pieces of them anyway, strewn across the ground. An arm lay not two feet away from my head inside the tent and I felt myself start to shake from shock.

It wasn't *like* my nightmare. It was my

nightmare *exactly*.

I could see through the torn tent flaps to where Buzz and Dark looked to be examining pieces of carcasses scattered in the snow. They walked from piece to piece in the stained snow that was various shades of blood red to pink. They both turned and nodded at me as they continued about the area.

Cormac went around to my feet as I pulled my free wrists in front of me and rubbed them. I looked down to where he was trying to cut away blood-encrusted rope from my ankles. It was my blood this time, caked into where the rope dug into my skin.

Cormac looked behind him to where Dark and Dodd were a good distance away, then back to me. "Do you remember any of it?" His voice was soft, not like he was particularly looking to keep the question quiet but wasn't looking to broadcast it either.

"Just remnants." And that was enough.

My hands shook as I tried to raise the water bottle he'd left by my side to my mouth.

He came around and steadied my hand. "Do you remember how you did it?"

"I don't think I did."

I let him take the bottle when I would have chugged it.

"They didn't do it for food. The bodies are torn

apart but all the torsos and heads are there." He kneeled by my side. "They didn't do this on their own." His eyes were saying more and I didn't like any of it.

"I was knocked out. How could I have ordered it?"

I started shaking in earnest then and made a futile attempt to get to my feet but I could barely get to my knees.

"How long was I out for?"

"Three days." He reached down and picked me up.

"I'm filthy," I said, embarrassed that he was seeing me, let alone touching me.

He didn't let go but held me closer to him.

"Did they feed you or give you water at all?"

I shook my head. "I don't think so."

"They could've killed you." There was constrained rage in his voice.

"How did you find me?" I rested my head on his shoulder, exhausted in spite of not being awake for days.

"We didn't. The rippers found us and led us here."

We walked out of the tent, me in Cormac's arms. I tried to look at Buzz and Dark, but I was having a hard time keeping my eyes open in the glaring light.

"Did you ID them?" he asked as he walked

toward the truck that was waiting close by.

"Yeah, what should we do with the bodies?" Buzz asked.

"Leave them for the vultures to pick at their bones. Whatever doesn't get eaten can lie here rotting. Let's go."

He climbed in to the backseat, me still in tow. He reached for a thick blanket on the seat next to us and tucked it in around me.

I fell asleep before Buzz and Dark even got back in the truck.

***

"There you are."

I was surrounded by warmth as a towel ran up and down my arm. Opening my eyes, I saw Cormac lean over me as I reclined in a bath of hot water. An empty IV bag hung in the corner.

"Trying to rehydrate you while you were sleeping. The drugs are still working out of your system. You were pretty pumped up with them so it might take a while to feel normal." His hand dropped the towel in the water again.

"Did anyone see me?" It wasn't vanity that concerned me, I'd spent months asserting myself over a crowd that didn't take to authority. I didn't want them to see me looking weak.

"I brought you in through a back entrance while

Dark and Dodd created a diversion at the front."

His eyes roved over my body and instead of being uncomfortable or pushing him away, I met his eyes with a look of my own.

One hand slipped behind my head as he lowered his lips to mine. When I thought it would go further, he pulled back.

"What do you remember?"

I leaned my head back on the rim of the tub. I replayed all the memories up until they showed up.

His hand ran over my head, pushing the hair out of my face while he waited patiently for me to finish.

"I thought it was a dream. I heard the screaming and the crying but I didn't think it was real."

"Do you remember trying to call the rippers to you?"

"I told you, I don't think I did. I was out of my mind with the drugs."

"Cormac?" It was Dodd's voice from the living room.

"I'll be right there. You okay?" he asked as he stood from his squatting position by the bath.

"Yes."

"I'll be back in a few minutes."

I watched as he headed toward the door and the memories replayed in my mind.

"Cormac?"

He turned and paused, one foot out of the bathroom.

"We need to call a castle meeting. It's coming. They need to know."

His hand gripped the door and his face lost all the tenderness that was there a moment ago.

"I agree. They do."

Chapter Fourteen

Just a Small Affair

The meeting signs had been posted for that night, at my insistence. Cormac had argued that I should give myself another day to get on my feet but I couldn't. Now that I knew it was happening, and probably sooner than I had expected, I just needed to tell them. As if until I spoke the words out loud, and to everyone, they would chew away at what was left of my sanity.

The senator is coming. Everyone had been waiting for it. It wouldn't be a surprise but I still needed to say it for everyone to hear.

I walked with purpose and a heavy step as I entered the great hall. All heads turned to me and it looked like every single person in residence had shown, crammed into the room and overflowing into the nearby hallways. They knew. Maybe they weren't sure, but they suspected. I guess, on some level, we'd all been waiting for this moment.

Without thought, I scanned the room for Cormac. He stood next to the small platform I'd asked him to erect. Being short, I wanted to make sure I could see everyone's faces, and they could see mine when I told them. I wanted to be able to look them in the eye. They deserved that.

Everyone parted as I made my way over and stepped up on the platform. The crowd, eager to know what news caused such an unusual gathering, immediately hushed.

"Thank you for coming." I scanned the hall, taking in all the faces. I knew all of them, even if I didn't recall every name. There was nothing but furrowed brows and concerned expressions, and again, I felt the weight of the news pressing down upon me. I was suddenly afraid I wouldn't be able to say what I needed to.

Maybe I should have had Cormac tell them, but they deserved to hear it from me. Most didn't care for me anyway, which was why I was the best person to deliver the news. They already hated the messenger, no more harm done.

"I know most of you have heard of the senator." A murmur ripped through the crowd, and I ignored it. "There have been rumors of a war coming." The crowd grew restless at that and I took a deep breath, and plunged in before I lost them, and my nerve. "That war is now imminent."

The crowd instantly erupted. Questions were screamed, everyone vying to be heard over their neighbor until no one was audible. Cormac edged in a hair closer on one side and Dark on my other, waiting for the crowd to lose control. I could see by their positions, they were preparing for trouble. That's when I noticed the strategic positions of the other Keepers in the room. They were slowly moving in closer to the platform and me. They thought it could turn violent, that was how fierce the energy was.

"People!" I shouted, hoping all the non-humans wouldn't take that as an insult. "Please, calm down!" I needed to get them under control. All it took was one to lose control and all hell could break loose.

Then I saw Burrom off in the back corner. He was staring at me like I should be doing something. But what?

He lifted a hand and waved his finger around as if swirling it in an invisible stew.

Maybe not so invisible.

I raised my hands as if to nonverbally ask the crowd to calm down, but that wasn't what I was doing at all. More than half of the occupants in the room were magical beings. As such, they emitted magical energy. If I could pull the angry energy of the room into myself, perhaps I could avert a mob scene.

Slowly, I felt it trickle to me. Gradually, the noise in the room dropped a hair. This would work. I steadily pulled more and the crowd calmed more.

I just needed to channel it somewhere. That was the trick. I'd held too much it last time and needed to divert it out into something else.

I noticed Burrom approaching along the side of the room where Dark stood. What was he doing? He passed by Dark and behind the podium set up in front of me and grabbed my hand. I looked quickly at him and he nodded.

"It could kill you," I said, but I knew I had to do something quick. The colors of the magic were starting to shimmer in the air, only visible to me, as they had last time right before I'd overloaded.

"Do it."

I felt my other hand being grabbed and realized Cormac had taken it. I hadn't realized he'd even been aware of what was going on.

Cormac squeezed my hand. He still wasn't looking at me but keeping his eye on the crowd. "Split it between us."

I let the power flow through me and felt them both tense at the onslaught of pure magical energy pulsing into them. I broke contact as soon as I felt the pressure subside from me and the colors dim. It was just enough to get me out of the danger zone, I hoped.

Cormac turned, eyed me skeptically and tried to grab my hand again.

"No."

"Yes," he said and grabbed my hand but to no use. I'd shut down the connection and he wasn't strong enough to pull it from me if I wasn't willing to give it.

The crowd hushed enough for me to hear a woman call out a single question. "When?"

And silence fell as that was probably the most important question at hand.

I held her gaze, speaking directly to her. "We don't have an exact date, but he's organizing now."

"Are you sure?" another man, one of the *changed,* asked. At least I thought he was a man. Completely covered in a shaggy grey fur, it wasn't easy to tell.

"Yes. Sure enough that I felt you all needed to be told. I don't make this statement lightly."

"Why? I'd heard there was a truce?" A different woman in the back asked.

"There was a truce. It looks like he's going to break it."

"What do we do?" This question came from several people.

I gripped the sides of the podium in front of me.

"As I see it, there are two choices. You can leave here and try to find somewhere else to go. Or, you can stay and fight with us."

People started frantically talking amongst themselves.

"But, know one thing. If you stay, you fight." I spoke louder to make sure everyone heard.

"Even the children?"

I hadn't thought about the children. "Well, no. Not the little ones."

"What about the injured or unable?"

"Of course not."

Another person in the back raised their hand.

"Yes?"

"I get panic attacks. Does that count?"

"I don't know. Can you still function?"

"I hyperventilate sometimes."

"Yeah, me too!"

I let out a deep sigh, annoyed, and wondered if Cormac had been up here if they would've asked these questions.

"Enough. Anybody who can fight, has to. Carry a brown paper bag, if that's what it takes. You have a week to decide."

I stepped past Cormac and exited the room, thinking about how fucked we were if this was any sign.

I walked straight out the lobby doors and then sprinted down the strip. As they'd spoken, I'd continued to pull more energy from the room and I was teetering on the edge. I needed to get rid of it and I needed no one to be around when I unleashed it.

I turned in a circle, looking for any innocent bystanders, slightly frantic now in my need to expel the power coursing through me before it could possibly kill me. I didn't know what would happen when I let it go, but I had to. Alone and acting on instinct, eyes closed, I opened my mouth, spread out my arms and pushed it from my system, outward into the area around me. I finally felt it all release and my body felt like my own again.

I opened my eyes, hoping I hadn't caused a building to crumple or some other sort of additional destruction. I gasped at the sight as I looked down at what used to be the Vegas strip. There were hundreds of rippers standing as far as I could see.

They weren't all opaque either. Some of them, like when they first started to appear, were slightly translucent. Were more still coming? And for the very first time, I feared I might have something to do with it. This might not be reassuring to all the people I was trying to recruit to fight with me.

I didn't know what to do as they all were approaching. It was a long shot, but maybe, if I just left they would go away. It was a ridiculous idea, but stupider things had worked. I choked back the nervous laughter that was welling up and realized I might be starting to crack under the pressure. This seemed to make it even funnier to me, perhaps confirming the conclusion.

I turned to rush into the casino and stopped short.

I saw the *changed,* all standing in front of the castle. Colleen, Sharon, Katie, Evan, the whole gang was there, with Cormac standing front and center.

I knew it didn't look good but I held my head up and kept walking.

"How did you do that?" he asked as I came closer.

I thought he meant the rippers. I could still hear their careening floating on the wind as they remained where they were.

I looked back to the rippers, who seemed to be glued in place. There was no denying it was me somehow, but I simply shook my head as to an explanation.

When I turned back to him and saw his face, I knew Cormac was stunned. Nothing stunned Cormac.

"Not them. Us." The weight he put on the word 'us' was like a cinder block dropping into a pool and heavily thudding to the bottom.

"What do you mean?" I understood what he said but I couldn't get my head around the reality of what it meant.

He was staring at me oddly. The rest of the *changed* were speechless.

I still didn't understand the how of it.

"You called us." He said this with absolute certainty.

"No, I didn't call for you." I shook my head in disagreement.

But he just kept at it. "Yes. You did."

And then he threw me a lifeline and I grabbed it with both hands.

Chapter Fifteen

The Cycle of Life

When Cormac ordered me to the penthouse, I took it for the favor it was and scrambled out of there. I didn't care if it hurt my pride. I saw the look in his eyes and recognized it. Neither of us knew what just happened. And as much as I rode him about how he handled things, him ordering me inside at that very moment was a knee jerk reaction to buy me time. When he didn't know how else to accomplish it, he fell back on his autocratic ways.

My pride be damned, I'd rushed inside, quite happy to take that order. Of course, I didn't have any intention of going to the penthouse. I didn't think Cormac even cared. I knew the dictate had been to save my ass from the questions about to hit from every side.

Answers? I didn't have answers for them. I didn't know myself. Instead of admitting that, which might have freaked them all out more, Cormac and Colleen had stepped up and started doing damage control. I didn't even know what they were going to say, but it allowed me to duck out of there for a minute and shake off the shock of what I'd just done.

My entire body felt weak from the drugs still

lingering in my system. The calling every ripper in the area, while calling to every *changed* as well, certainly didn't help matters.

Maybe I needed sleep. I didn't have time to rest but I was going to have to, if I wanted to be coherent. I couldn't even think straight anymore and I'd need a clear mind to come up with a plausible explanation for what I'd done.

I also didn't have time to worry about it right now. No one did. If it wasn't an imminent threat, it needed to go on the back burner. We needed to get enlistment signup sheets tomorrow and start trying to squeeze out every ounce of fighting power we could. I didn't know how many we were up against, but I was sure the numbers would be greater than ours.

I needed to talk to Dodd. I couldn't afford to have Sabrina holed up in his room anymore. She'd just have to get over it. We'd all had horrible things happen. It was time to suck it up.

As I walked down the hallway, it was pretty quiet; most people were either in the great hall gossiping about the meeting, or outside gossiping about the latest sideshow production. They were probably trying to pump Cormac for more information. With everything that was on my mind, it hadn't even occurred to me that Buzz hadn't been at the meeting until he was sprinting toward me from the opposite direction of the hall.

"What's wrong?"

"You gotta come to Dodd's, right now." He was breathing heavily, a sheen of sweat on his forehead.

I started running for Dodd's before I asked another question. Buzz was trailing too far behind and I didn't wait for him to catch up as I took the stairs two at a time. My lungs burning, my fist pounded on the antique wooden door.

It was yanked open by a strung out looking Dodd. He was a Keeper. It took a lot for a Keeper to look haggard. I'd just been kidnapped, deprived of food and water for three days, called a mass of man-eating monsters to me while simultaneously calling every *changed* in the area, and I still looked better than him. Actually, thinking about it made me want to go collapse on my bed.

He didn't stop to talk but wrapped a hand around my arm and dragged me in with him into his bedroom. If I hadn't known what was going on and that Sabrina was there, I might have gotten a hair worried that he'd gone off the reservation. I would never admit it, but that's how bad he looked. He was bordering on creepy. If I'd seen him as a stranger walking down the street, I would've ducked into a crowded store to avoid getting close to him.

Once I saw what awaited me, I was grateful for it too, because if he hadn't been propelling me forward I might have sunk to the ground the minute I crossed the threshold.

Sabrina, or at least I thought the creature was Sabrina, was in the middle of the bed. If I hadn't seen the beginning of her transformation, I wouldn't have known her. Blue-green scales covered the top half of her head like a strange masquerade mask. She lay upon wings outstretched beneath her. Her hands were clawed, as well as her bare feet. Her limbs, which had once been graceful and feminine, were all just sinew without an ounce of fat to soften the tendons and muscles that bulged.

I'd noticed the room was darker than even the stone normally made it and then I looked around and saw the same black marks on the walls. They looked identical to the ones we had found at the energy plant, the place Rulagh had lived.

My eyes met hers and I wanted to speak, but what could I possibly say? Her eyes, the only thing left of the Sabrina I knew, looked tortured and my heart broke.

She let out a freakish howl, lifted her head back and a burst of fire shot from her mouth. She gripped her stomach, a very rounded stomach and the pieces clicked into place. This was the hiding and the torment I'd sensed whenever Dodd mentioned her. She was like Rulagh now, and I feared what she might be carrying. I thought of my foolish idea that I'd be able to fix her with *my time to get up and go on* pep talk. This situation was way beyond my rehearsed "suck it up" material.

Her whimpers finally kicked me into gear and I rushed to kneel by her side. I gripped her...hand? She was lying there in pain and I forced myself out of the frozen and mute stage.

"Sabrina, what's happening?"

A steady trail of tears ran down her cheeks as she finally turned to me.

"I'm a monster. I didn't want Dodd to call anyone."

"No, you're not. You couldn't be. Not you." I squeezed my grip in reassurance and forced myself to run a hand over the scales on her forehead. "You could have come to me. I would've been there for you."

Her body tensed in visible pain. "It's coming," she said.

I didn't ask what, I was afraid to confirm whose, and I was beyond trying to count days since nothing about this was normal. She wasn't human, anymore. A nine month term pregnancy probably didn't apply. I could deal with not knowing who, but as I tried to move into position to help her try and deliver it, having an idea *what* would've have been a really nice thing to know.

"Dodd?" I looked around the room to find him standing just behind me. "Get water and blankets. Oh, and a knife or scissors. And some kind of clamp as well." He ran off to go do my bidding and I looked at Sabrina, hoping I had covered all the

bases. She was the doctor after all. I only knew
what I'd seen on TV shows.

"Yes, that's good," she said, as she tried to
wriggle up into a half sitting position. I moved to
help her before preparing to assess the situation.

I was just about to see if I could determine how
far along her labor was, when Sabrina clasped my
hand that was on her knee.

"Jo?" Her hand squeezed tightly on mine and I
noted the change had definitely made her stronger
than normal.

"Don't worry. I know I've never done this
before but I'm a really quick study."

She shook her head. "That's not it. There's
something wrong."

I held back my sarcastic response of *what could
possibly be wrong*? Even I knew it was out of place
and being driven by fear and nerves.

I decided to go with, "Why do you say that?"

"I'm a doctor." She leaned back, anxiety in her
eyes. "This isn't normal."

"What do you think is wrong?"

"Jo, I'm hundreds of years old. Even Keeper
females run out of eggs. I shouldn't have been able
to get pregnant." She stared at me, daring me to
continue pretending this was anything close to
normal.

I nodded and tried to infuse my voice with
confidence. "Whatever happens, I will get you

through this."

"Promise me something?"

"Anything," I said but inwardly cringed.

What else was I supposed to say? Deathbed promises are a bitch. For all I knew, there was a heaven, and all those people who asked for favors right when they knew they couldn't be turned down are probably skipping around fancy free. Meanwhile, all of us who agreed are loaded down with all sorts of crap we never would've agreed to under normal circumstances. Seriously, any negotiations under these terms should be null and void. I knew it was a valid point, but I wasn't going to be the ass to say, hey, I only agreed because she was dying.

"Promise to take care of it."

"What about Dodd?"

When she looked off to the side, I knew my last escape was about to take a leap out the window and die a painful but quick death.

"It's not Dodd's. Rulagh raped me."

I nodded. "I promise."

And that's when the bad thoughts started. It wasn't that I didn't love Sabrina and feel horrible about what was going on, BUT there she'd be, dancing through pearly gates while I had to babysit Godzilla out of misplaced guilt. If there was a fuck my life charter club, I'd officially be president right now.

When we heard the commotion in the other room, I felt her pulse pick up even faster.

"Stay calm. I'll get rid of them and be right back." I gave her a pat, the situation seemed to call for something of the sort, and I rushed out of the bedroom, shutting the door behind me. Cormac, Buzz and Dark were arguing with Dodd, who carried my supplies.

"What the hell is going on?" Cormac asked as soon as I stepped in the room.

"I don't have time right now." I grabbed the supplies from Dodd.

When Cormac made to follow me, I held up a hand to hold him off as I managed to juggle my stuff. "No. She's already stressed. Dodd will have to explain. No one comes in unless explicitly invited by her."

Dodd took a step next to me, physically backing up my words.

"You going to tell me what's going on?" Cormac asked, offering a silent compromise, information for cooperation. I'd seen how quick Cormac could really move. If he pushed the issue, I didn't think either Dodd or I'd be able to keep him out of the room. Actually, I knew we couldn't.

"Hurry up," I said to Dodd before I left them to go back into the bedroom. I was protecting her privacy, but it wasn't like I wanted to be in there alone.

"Who's out there?" Sabrina asked as I settled back near the bed.

"Dodd, Cormac and Buzz, but Dodd is keeping them out."

It looked like she was about to say something but instead, whatever it initially was turned into a scream as she was wracked with another contraction. I looked down, expecting to see something, hopefully a head. I was relieved when it did seem to be that. She must have seen the emotions and fear on my face.

"What?" she asked, in between contractions.

"Nothing. Everything is fine. Just breathe deep." And I needed to school my expressions better. Once upon a time, I'd had a great poker face.

"How's she doing?" Dodd asked, coming in and perching on the side of the bed near Sabrina. He held her hand as he looked to me.

"She's doing great." I watched as Sabrina sank back into the bed and closed her eyes in exhaustion. "How long has this been going on?"

"All day, but she hid it. I didn't know about it until an hour ago."

I nodded my head in the direction of the living room.

He looked at her and then back to me, and mouthed the words, *I told them but I asked them to stay out there.*

I might need help. I widened my eyes in

emphasis.

Sabrina's eyes snapped open again as she cried out in agony and I watched as a small human head pushed out a few more centimeters. When Sabrina collapsed again, I started to fear she wouldn't make it. She looked much weaker even than when I'd arrived. I felt her wrist, which lay limp on the side of the bed opposite Dodd. The pulse was weak and thready.

"I'll be right back," I said.

Dodd nodded as he wiped the hair from Sabrina's scaled forehead.

I found Cormac pacing the living room.

"Where's Dark and Buzz?"

"I sent them to find Burrom. Desperate times and all that." He walked closer to me to make sure he couldn't be heard in the other room. "How's it going?"

"Something's wrong. She's weaker than she should be. I know she's in labor," I couldn't even begin to tell him that I feared what might be coming out of her, "but she's too weak. Her pulse is getting faint. She's a Keeper. Shouldn't she be able to handle giving birth? Shouldn't she be able to heal whatever is going wrong?"

"Maybe not." He scratched his shadowed jaw in contemplation and then rested his hands on his hips.

"Why not?" It was the last thing I wanted to

hear.

"Because, when a woman gives birth, there are certain things that have to happen in order for labor to occur. Keeper's bodies shut down our healing until after they deliver."

"How much after?" I watched as he sat down on Dodd's couch and I didn't like the look of things. I would have preferred pacing.

"Depends. It's very individual. I've heard of it happening minutes after to sometimes days after."

"You're saying she could die during labor?"

He rested his elbows on his knees and his chin on his fist.

"It's why I'm having them look for Burrom. Maybe he knows a trick we don't."

He spoke when I turned to leave. "Do you want me to come in there with you?"

I knew Dodd asked him to stay out because of Sabrina's wishes, but I wanted him to walk back in the room and take over. I just didn't know how to face what might be coming, but when I heard her cry, I went in alone.

Another four hours passed and whatever it was that was going to come out hadn't moved. She was barely coherent at this point, and then it was only right after she was ripped back into awareness and screaming in pain.

All thoughts to maintaining her privacy went out the window an hour ago as Cormac, Burrom,

Dodd, Buzz, Dark, Colleen, Sharon and Katie were all piled in the apartment and taking turns by the bedside with me.

I got up and stretched my legs in between a contraction. "What do we do?" I heard Dark ask from the other room as I stood by the door.

"I've no idea why you all thought I'd have some knowledge of this." That was Burrom. He'd been the last to arrive. We'd a hard time finding him initially as he'd been otherwise occupied with a female *changed,* having sex in the dungeons. Dark had offered to elaborate on how he'd found him but I asked him to spare me the details.

Sabrina's screams turned to moans as another contraction forced her back into consciousness. I rushed back into place by her as she bore down with Dodd's help. The head that had been struggling to come out finally emerged. Another push and I was able to pull the shoulders out afterward.

A beautiful little baby boy lay in my hands and let out an angry cry that filled the room. I looked up to congratulate Sabrina but she wasn't stirring.

"Sabrina?"

And then I saw the blood start to pool underneath her. She was hemorrhaging and badly. I placed the baby by her side as I tried to press towels to her, knowing it was futile.

"Cormac!" I screamed to the other room.

He was by my side in a second but he didn't do

anything when he saw the blood filled rags I held to her, trying anything to staunch the bleeding.

"Help me!"

"There's nothing I can do." He placed a hand on my shoulder and shook his head. "It's too heavy."

I looked down back to where the blood was now pooling again, in spite of the towels.

I didn't know what to say. Dodd's eyes didn't look at the baby as I clamped off the cord and swaddled him. His eyes never left Sabrina.

The three of us watched as she quickly slipped further away from us. What skin she had left was ashen. She was dying. There was no arguing about it now, even if she did have enough awareness. I didn't know if I should try and rouse her or if I should just let her be in peace.

"Dodd..." I started. I reached out my free hand to him but he shook his head, still not looking anywhere but her. My arms filled with Rulagh and Sabrina's son, I realized there would be no talking to him.

And then I heard it, a death rattle. Sabrina was gone and Dodd wasn't really there anymore, either.

He dropped her hand and left the room without a word. I heard them try and stop him as he passed through the living room, right before the door slammed.

I walked into the living room and tried to find a way to explain that Sabrina had passed. When I saw

their faces, I realized words weren't necessary.
Dodd's exit had said it all.

Chapter Sixteen

Compromising Promises

"Do you think it was okay to leave the baby with Dark?" I watched Cormac's face while he opened the door to the penthouse. He rested against it, waiting for me to walk past. There was a look in his eyes that put my senses on edge, as if every drop of his attention was focused solely on me.

"He wanted to take him tonight and he's great with the kids. He'll find a wet nurse. There are a couple of women that had babies recently, even if they just handle the feedings."

I felt the death of Sabrina deeply and I'd only known her less than a year. He'd known her for centuries. But, then again, sometimes it's not how long you've known someone but how well. We'd all gone through hell together and it was almost sad how much stronger the bad times bonded you then the good, welded you together by the heat of brimstone.

"You're running on empty. You need a break," he said.

I threw him a look that replied I wasn't the only one.

It was late and the only light in the penthouse was from the fireplace giving a warm glow to the room. I settled down onto the couch, not ready to sleep, my thoughts still spinning. He sat down on the opposite side of the same couch, facing me.

I leaned my head along the back and waited.

"What happened outside? Where did all those rippers come from?"

"I needed to get rid of some of the magical energy. I went to a clear area and pushed it out. When I opened my eyes, you, the rippers, and the *changed* were all there. You said I called you, but I don't remember doing anything to call any of you, or the rippers."

I pulled my knees to my chest and wrapped my arms around them.

"I was just leaving the hall when it happened. It was like a beacon, calling me to your spot. I looked around and I saw every *changed* in the area perk up, and I knew we were all feeling it." His arm reached in my direction along the back of the couch, and even though we weren't talking about us, the tension hung in the air.

"I don't have an explanation."

"I know. I noticed the surprise on your face when you saw us. By the way, were you really going to try and just sneak back in?"

"Maybe?" A nervous giggle slipped out and lightened the mood slightly. "What happened to you all these months? Where did you go?"

It was the first real opening I'd given him to

discuss what had happened. I felt beaten down by the fresh loss of Sabrina and all my ideas about being strong and staying separate from him didn't seem to matter anymore. I wanted comfort.

I watched him and waited, hoping he would say something that I could live with. I was done looking for perfection, I just needed something that I could hang my hat on, that would let me forgive him.

He ran his hand through his hair, looking as tired as me for once.

"Do you remember the day before I left?"

Of course I did. I could recall every second of that day. I'd replayed those moments over and over again. I thought back to that time, shortly after the influx of new Fae and wolves. It had been a blur of activity but I remembered every word, action and gesture. How many times had I tried to analyze what went wrong?

I wouldn't admit to that so I shrugged, trying to make less of it than it was. "What about it?"

"Do you remember the last time in the conference room?"

"Yes."

I played with a loose thread on my pants. How could I forget? Burrom had just left the room and Cormac followed him to the door, I thought to say a few final words, until he shut it and locked it. He'd walked to me and I hadn't been sure what he was about to do until he was tearing my clothes off and pressing into me the next second. The only word for it was primal.

"I wasn't myself."

"It sure felt like you."

"I was out of control."

"I didn't think you were that different than you were any of the other times." There was always something animalistic about being with Cormac.

"The other times, I could have chosen to pull back. When I threatened Vitor in that meeting, if he hadn't backed down, I would've have killed him. I wasn't thinking, I was reacting."

"Where did you go when you left?"

"I went out into the desert, where there were no humans, just rippers. Then I stopped fighting the changes, and completely relinquished control." His face was in deep concentration. "I don't even remember the first two months."

"Nothing?"

"When I think back, there are small snippets, but most of it is just gone."

"You said the first two months, but what about the last?"

He leaned forward a bit.

"After the first two months, I woke up one morning completely coherent. My clothes were ripped to shreds. There were a few dead, bloodied ripper bodies around me but I was aware."

"I still don't understand what happened. Why

you did this." I leaned forward in the darkly lit room and stared at his face, searching for answers.

"In the beginning, when it first happened, I'd felt the magic gnawing at me. I'd manage to keep it at bay, to remain in control. I was afraid if I let it in, who knew what I could become. You've seen what it does to some people."

Neither of us spoke Sabrina's name, but nonetheless, it was there in the room with us.

"I'd fought it for so long that when the wave of magic swept in that last time it opened, I knew I was done. I was slipping. I could feel myself reacting and I had almost no control over what I was doing."

"But you're okay now?" I needed him to be.

"I feel different, but in control."

"So it's done? You're normal now?"

"Sort of."

I wrapped my arms a little tighter around my legs, not overly reassured by that description.

"You don't need to be alarmed. I'm still me, just…more."

"How?" I'd already recognized some of the changes but I wanted to hear it from him.

"Like you guessed a while ago, I don't need to sleep. That was one of the first changes. My body regenerates while I'm awake. My cells and tissues are denser which makes me harder to hurt, and I hear better. I'm everything I used to be, but somehow more."

"How do you disappear?"

He laughed a little. "I don't really disappear. I can push my body to speeds that are hard to see in small bursts."

"But you're okay now? You aren't going to go crazy again?" What I really wanted to ask was you aren't going to leave again. At the heart of it, it was the question I needed the answer to most.

"No." He'd slowly moved closer to me as we'd talked. His one arm was relaxed on the back of the couch as his other hand started to rub my bent leg. I watched it move up and down, not sure what I was going to do.

"I waited another month just to make sure I was in control again, that I wouldn't be a danger to you."

His hand, now near my hip, slowly slipped downward again, wrapped around my ankle, pulling my leg straight until my right calf was flush against his hip. His palm then moved further up my leg until it was gripping my hip, his other hand supporting himself as he leaned forward.

I pressed my palm against his chest. "Cormac." Everything I was feeling was wrapped into his name.

His hand pushed a blond lock out of my face and he rubbed the back of his fingers along my cheek.

"I didn't want to leave you."

I kept the tension in my arm, not pushing him away, but slowing him when he would've pressed in further.

"How do I know it won't happen again?" I needed something, anything. I couldn't knowingly go through that again.

His eyes grew sad and the corner of his lips turned down. "You don't. Nobody knows what will happen. The only thing I can promise is that I won't do it because I want to leave you. I never wanted to leave you."

He moved in closer and tugged my hips, pulling me snug beneath his. I didn't push him off of me but I kept my hands flat on his chest between us.

"I begged you to not leave." I looked up at his face, willing him to give me something to hang on to. Anything.

"I know it was hard for you."

I hadn't shared my feelings with anyone. It had crushed me but I'd suffered alone.

He must have read my expression.

"People talk. You can't always hide what you're going through."

I turned my head and pushed at him embarrassed that while he'd thought of nothing for two months, I'd barely held myself together. And according to unknown sources, I hadn't done it very well. "Get off. I want to get up." But he didn't budge.

His chest pressed down against me as his hands cupped my face, forcing me to look at him.

"Jo, the very second I became myself again, all I thought of was getting back to you. Do you really want to give up what we have because of fear? Control is only an illusion. I could sit here and tell you we'll be together forever, but I'd be lying. No one knows what will be. Don't throw this away." His thumb ran along my jaw as his mouth dipped down and nibbled at my lips before he retreated again. "I've lived thousands of years and never felt like this." He dipped his head again, his body fitting firmer to mine. "I didn't know I *could* feel like this." His left hand reached down and under the back of my knee, arching it up. His grip ran down the length of my thigh before stopping at my hip.

"I need you." His voice was aching and raw and undid me.

"Promise me you won't leave."

"But I told you..."

"Promise me."

He froze. "I would do it again if I thought I might hurt you."

"Promise me." The feelings between us were quickly changing from heated passion, to anger on my part and frustration on his. "I can't be with someone that is going to disappear on me. I have enough issues." I pushed hard, sliding myself upward and he moved off of me.

"I can't make that promise." He spoke through a clenched jaw as he stood up, putting distance between us.

"You need to."

"Hey." We both turned to see Dark standing in the door with the baby.

"Do you ever knock anymore?" I knew the terseness in his voice was for me even though he was speaking to Dark.

"Dude, I live here now. This baby is making all sorts of crazy noises. It's freaking me out." His concern for the kid seemed to overrule any trepidation Dark had about interrupting.

Cormac walked over and took the swaddled baby, which Dark gingerly handed over.

"Anybody see Dodd yet?" You had to listen very closely but there was an undertone to Cormac's voice that I recognized. He was more concerned about Dodd than he wanted to let on. It could only mean one thing; he thought there was a chance Dodd wouldn't be back.

"No. Crash said he hit them up for some of the special ammo and disappeared." Dark shoved his free hands into his pockets and rocked on his heels.

My heart squeezed a little as I saw how the baby didn't cry or fuss at all now that Cormac was cradling him.

"He's upset," I said. "He's probably just blowing off some steam."

"Go see if you can find him," Cormac said to Dark. "Find Chip. He might be able to help."

Cormac walked back into the room as Dark took off.

"He needs time."

Cormac sat on the couch with the baby. "He doesn't get to have time. We need everyone."

I pulled my legs up underneath me and refused to believe we might not see Dodd again.

"We don't know how many people the senator has and we've got thousands here capable of fighting."

He lowered his eyes but I saw the dread in them before he did.

"Do you know something?" I angled myself, trying to catch his evasive stare. "Cormac. What do you know?"

"They're already packing."

"Who?"

"From the sounds of it? More than half the castle. Every Fae that is immune to the rippers and every wolf as well."

"What about the *changed*?"

"Not that I've heard. They look like they are staying, at least for now."

I got to my feet, as he stayed seated with the baby.

"Where are you going?"

"I have to see for myself." Months of busting

my ass trying to keep everyone fed and safe and things get a little rough and they pack their bags less than a day later?

"Want me to go with you? I'll call Colleen to watch him." He nodded down to the baby in his arms.

"I need to do this on my own." I needed to do this alone. Maybe it was because he wouldn't promise to stay. It could've been that I was the one who for three months worried about how I was going to keep everything together for them. If they were leaving, it would hit me somewhere deep inside and I wasn't ready to share the experience.

He nodded, a look I took to be understanding in his eyes.

Chapter Seventeen

Every Man for Himself

I stepped into Vitor's domain. It was the third floor I'd visited in the last fifteen minutes and it was the exact same scene as the other two that held the wolves. Doors were opening as people came and went, hustling to pack their boxes in what looked to be a mass exodus.

I took the well-worn path to Vitor's suite. The door was wide open but I tapped on it anyway to announce my arrival.

His gaze flew to me, then turned back to the three Fae next to him and he motioned to the door. They looked from him to me and nodded, exiting quickly.

I heard the door close quietly behind me as I took in the room. Drawers and closets were open and empty, their contents piled into boxes or in neat little stacks as they waited to be packed.

"I kept your sister here, and all the other Fae refugees, when we were overflowing with too many mouths to feed and very little room left. This is how you repay me?" I asked, my voice starting to rise by the end.

There was fractional dropping of his head, but his resolute expression didn't falter.

"It's what's best for my people."

I shook my head as I took a few steps around the room.

"And they don't owe me some sort of allegiance? They weren't fed, clothed and housed here?" I clenched my fists to stop myself from knocking over one of his packed boxes in anger.

"If feels like a lifetime ago when I first met you, so beautiful and naive walking through the Lacard mall. Even then, I could see the woman you would become. It could've been so different between us, but you chose him. Then he left you and I waited, thinking you'd finally see the light, but the moment he came back, I saw you and I knew you'd end up right back with him."

"So, you're leaving because I don't want to be with you? That's what you are saying?"

"These are my people. Their survival is all I can concern myself with. I'm not sure what would have happened if you'd made different choices. All I do know is you made it easy for me." He turned and started to place a few things in an open box sitting on the table, silently ending our conversation.

I walked from the room, wondering if I'd ever see him again. I made my way to the stairwell, as Fae darted quickly out of my path and avoided any eye contact. I paused, hand on the door that exited their area, and looked back down the long stretch of hallway. They all avoided eye contact but they were well aware of my presence still lingering. I cleared my throat and they slowed in their motions, wondering what I was about.

"If you leave here now, when I need you most, don't think, even for a second, you'll be welcome back."

The anxiety I just instilled into them was palpable. Good. I didn't want any denials that they didn't know the consequences.

My message sent and received, I pushed on the door, heading to my final stop.

***

Burrom's floor was eerily quiet, most of the rooms shut with very few people lingering in the hallways. I prepared myself for the worst as I raised my knuckles to his closed door. A heard a strange moan come from inside just as I knocked.

"Hang on!" I heard him yell.

The door swung open to reveal a naked Burrom. Okay, not exactly naked, but the teeny tiny towel hanging sinfully low on his hips covered just enough to keep the image from an R rating.

Yep, whatever I'd done at his burial ground months ago was seriously linked to my feelings for Cormac. His face might have resembled Cormac's brother, but the physique was identical.

"Like what you see?" He leaned back away

from the door, looking toward the entrance of his bedroom and then back to me. "I can kick them out if you want. Just give me five."

Them? "Not necessary. Where is everyone? Awfully quiet around here."

He smirked as he tipped his head toward me. "After all we've been through, Jo, you still don't trust me?"

The knot that had formed in my chest started to loosen up a bit.

"Where are they? Your people?"

"Partying like it's the end of the world, as per my orders. Babe, we might have agreed to go down with the ship but we're going out with some style." His eyes were big and his smile was bigger. "Okay, I'm not sure drunken drugged debauchery should be termed style, but we're really committed to doing this thing right."

"Do I want to know?"

"Just your typical end of the world stuff, you know, orgies, alcohol and heavy drug use. Nothing to fuss about. And don't worry, I told them that they absolutely weren't allowed to use farm animals or anyone unwilling."

"You had to tell them that? It needed to be said?" This was to be my army? The fate of what was left of the free world rested in these hands.

"I'm not a hundred percent sure it was necessary, but I figured it was safer that way. It's all in good fun." He tilted his head toward his room again. "If you aren't joining the party, do you mind? We were just getting to the good part."

I held up my palms, "Nope, not at all. You go."

He smiled again and went to shut the door but swung it back open quickly. "Oh, uh, I wouldn't breathe too deeply until you get off this floor."

"Got it."

Chapter Eighteen

The Cost of Sharing

"Are you really going to sit there all day and write names?" Cormac asked.

I was perched on a stone dragon that had shown up in the courtyard about a week ago. About ten feet off the ground, it was actually a pretty comfortable perch with good visuals. Its tail arched in a way that made a very ergonomic backrest and its head was the perfect height to rest my boots.

"Yes. I want to remember every single person that left. Who's got Harvey?" It was the name I'd started to call Sabrina's son. He was the last little piece of Sabrina and I didn't like to call him "it."

"Dark."

"I thought Dark was still freaked out after this morning." That was when we'd discovered Harvey wasn't as human as he appeared. After a bout of gas, we no longer had two couches in the penthouse. Dark had been holding Harvey at the time and lost a healthy chunk of hair to the fire burst he'd let loose during an especially loud burp.

"It was his turn. Everyone babysits the Harvey."

"In other words, you forced him."

"I can't have one of my men running around

afraid of a baby. It's embarrassing."

His hand reached up, resting on my thigh and I wasn't sure how to feel about it. We were in some weird relationship limbo land after last night. He'd been gone by time I'd gotten back and this was the first time I'd seen him.

I readjusted, using it as an excuse to dislodge the contact.

"We back there again?" he asked after removing his hand and leaning against the stone dragon.

"I can't instantly turn the feelings back on, especially when you can't make a commitment." I avoided eye contact, again. I was turning into such a wimp when it came to him.

"Did the feelings ever turn off?"

I ignored the question. "I didn't leave there. I can't move forward if I don't know where I'm going."

His expression was unreadable and also a place I didn't feel like going, so when I saw Buzz walking nearby, I hollered over to him.

"Can you believe this?" Buzz asked as he neared us. "Bunch of traitors."

"They're scared, is all," Cormac said.

"When did you become mister sensitive?" I asked.

"Since I learned what it feels like."

He was watching the mass exodus out of the

castle and I was grateful he wasn't paying attention to me. I wasn't sure I would've been able to hide how much that hit me.

I shoved my pad and pencil at Buzz. "Do me a favor? Write down all the names of anyone leaving?"

"On top of everything else I've got to do today?"

"I've got a lead on some Twix." Buzz had a crazy sweet tooth.

He grabbed the supplies. "Just names, or do you want times as well?"

"Names are fine."

I would've jumped down from my perch, but Cormac's hands found my waist as I slid down the front of him. My breathing shallow, my back arched of its own accord. He paused my descent just as I was eye to eye with him.

"Oh yeah, those feelings are buried really deep. I can tell." His voice was mocking as my cheeks burned.

"Do you mind? I've got work to do."

My feet hit the ground and I forced myself not to linger in his grasp.

"Where you going?"

"I've got to go find me some bugs to talk to."

***

"You didn't need to come," I said, not bothering to look at Cormac who was following me into the golf course where I'd last seen them.

"I'm quite aware that you have handled things very nicely while I've been gone."

"Then why are you following me?" I whipped around as I asked him.

"Because of this?" He pulled out what looked like two collars with little boxes on them.

"What are they?" I reached to take one from his hand but he lifted it too high.

"Oh no," he said smugly as he walked in front of me, putting the collars back in his pocket. "You aren't playing nice, so why should I share my toys?"

"Can you just tell me what they are?" I asked, following him through the snowy golf course.

"I think I'll need a show of goodwill."

"I haven't thrown your clothes out. I thought that was some amazing will." They'd been unpacked neatly in the closet, to my consternation, this morning. I'd had them packed away in a corner of the dungeons after he left. The only reason I hadn't thrown them out was I felt guilty knowing someone could use them. I was eventually going to give them away, but not until I could bear seeing his white shirts everywhere.

"It's a step." He paused and pulled out a single collar and held it out in front of him.

"Is that a camera?"

"Yes. I plan on convincing the owls to do a fly over while wearing these."

"Where did you get them?"

"I rigged some stuff up from the old pet supply place that was on the outskirts of town and collected some things from one of the camera stores that had a room still intact."

"This is fantastic," I said in an awed voice.

"And I bet you would love to see the footage if the owls agree." He was smirking, not even trying to hide his pleasure at having the upper hand.

"What do you want?"

He pocketed the collar and his hands reached down cupping my hips, he steered me back until I felt a tree at my back.

"Just a kiss."

I reached up and planted a quick kiss on his lips before pulling back.

"That's not a kiss." His eyes were hypnotic as they stared down at me. Under his stare, it felt like everything else in the world faded away. His lips moved slowly closer to mine. "This is a kiss."

He cupped my cheek, using his thumb to urge my face upward. He brushed his lips over mine with the barest of pressure. He nibbled slowly on my lower lip before his tongue briefly entered my mouth. The stiffness in my limbs dissolved and he took advantage of it by fitting my body to his.

Then the kiss deepened, all softness gone,

replaced by a possessiveness that shook me. I pressed my hands to his shoulders, breaking the contact and the intensity that sent me reeling. He pulled back enough to give me room but still kept contact.

"You got your kiss. Now let me see?" I asked.

"I kissed you. I'll share my toys, but I insist on an IOU for the kiss."

"Fine." If he'd known how rattled I was he might have pressed for a lot more, so I considered myself lucky.

He backed away with a smile and walked deeper into the golf course.

It took us another hour of calling before I found the bugs, not far from Burrom's tree, still in full foliage.

"Hi, Jo," the bugs greeted me and then a full minute later, they added "and him."

It was a little evil, the happiness I felt that at least somebody wasn't all enchanted with Cormac.

Pinky, the only one I could identify quickly because of the flashing pink on her tail, landed on my shoulder. "Do you know where the owls are?" I asked.

"They were around earlier. Don't know where they are now."

"Can you tell them I...we'd like to speak to them." Might as well use their adoration of Cormac to our benefit.

"Okay. Someone was looking for you."

"Who?" Cormac and I asked at the same moment.

"Weird old guy."

"Weird how?" Cormac asked.

"He was there but he wasn't there. And then he wasn't there at all."

Like the figure in the road before I crashed. I was really hoping for a mass hallucination. Sometimes crazy wasn't a bad thing. "Was he really big? What did he say?"

Fred flew over after making a couple zig zags due to his bent wing. "You're all big. He said 'Where's Jo?'"

"What did you reply?"

"We didn't know."

"Thanks. Please give the owls our message."

Cormac grabbed my hand and tugged me along.

"You know who it is?"

"I think it's got to be linked to the giant that showed up in the road then disappeared." I'd given Cormac a brief explanation about that night and I knew Colleen had filled in the gaps for him. "It would stand to reason that there aren't that many disappearing men floating around."

"I'm not sure I would take that for granted." He raised his brows as he said it.

"I don't have any other ideas."

"Could it be linked to the senator?"

"Every other time he wanted to talk to me, he's just come."

"How many times was that?" There was an edge to his voice as he asked.

"I don't know. I didn't count."

"More than a handful?"

"Yes, I guess."

"Why didn't you tell me this?"

"It didn't seem relevant."

"I have a feeling it's very relevant."

His grip was tightening painfully on my hand and his face was scowling.

"You're hurting me."

"Sorry," he said and immediately loosened his grip but didn't let go.

"What's got you so riled up?"

"The senator has a thing for you."

The idea was so ridiculous I smiled. "He hates me. Don't you remember the things he said to me?"

"Maybe that's how it started out," he stopped, forcing me to stop with him, "but I don't think those are his feelings now."

"Don't look at me like I had something to do with it."

"Did you lead him on? Maybe to keep the truce going?"

"How could you even ask me that?" I tried to wrench my hand out of his grasp but he didn't let go.

"It was a logical question since you've got half the casino sniffing after you."

"Including you?" I didn't know why I said it. Maybe because I still felt like he'd abandoned me, I wanted to rub it in a bit.

"Don't think for a second you can play me like the rest of your boys."

"My boys?"

His eyes hardened and before I could register alarm, his hand holding mine encircled my back and his other hand gripped my hair. I felt like I was in a storm as his lips pressed against mine, hard and demanding. It was a claiming kiss, one of possession mingled with jealousy.

When he let me go, I was reeling but tried to hide it. He started walking back in the direction of the casino. I didn't think he was going to speak again but I was wrong.

"You know what the most frustrating thing about this situation is?" He didn't wait for me to answer. "The old me wouldn't have worried about you. I would've done what I felt was best for my people and stayed at the castle, chips fall where they may. Wouldn't have worried about you getting hurt. I left because I cared. And not for Dodd or Dark or Sabrina, I left because I was worried about *you*. What would happen if I lost it while I lay next to you? I became the man you wanted me to be and you hate me for it."

Speechless, I watched his back as we walked. As we stepped into the castle, I still couldn't think of anything to say and I watched him walk away.

Chapter Nineteen

Skeleton Crew

When I finally fell asleep that night, after thinking all day about the ghost man who was lurking, and worse, Cormac's words, I fell asleep alone.

But I awoke with company. The tan muscular arm slung around my waist, hugging my back firmly to a warm and muscular chest. I was definitely not going to make the same mistake twice as I eyed the arm. I wouldn't make any sudden movements as I tried to decide if it was Burrom or Cormac.

Turning without alerting the man behind me seemed to be impossible, as snug as we were. I looked down at the hand, trying to examine it for some difference I could pick up on. I couldn't remember if Burrom wore any jewelry that might indicate whose it was, but Cormac didn't.

The arm pulled back giving me some room to assess the situation better. I turned and saw Cormac leaning against folded arms, very reminiscent of how Burrom had reclined there not long ago.

"Expecting someone else?"

My face must have given me away. "No." Maybe? "What time is it?"

"8:30."

"Shit!"

I jumped up ran across the room into the walk in closet. "Ugh! Your stuff is taking up all the room!"

"You mean my clothes in my closet, where they are supposed to be?"

I pushed past all the pristine shirts I had packed away and wondered where the hell he was getting them cleaned. How were they all still spotless?

"You are aware it's the end of the world, right? You could relax your dress code a bit? Maybe blend?" Only Cormac could remain well groomed in the apocalypse. "Sport a stain or two, just to look like you belong?"

"I've no desire to 'blend' anymore. By the way, you don't have to rush," he called from the other room as I yanked a clean sweatshirt over my head.

"Why?" I asked, half darting out and keeping my naked lower body behind the wall.

"I postponed it until nine-thirty."

A small part of me might have been annoyed he'd changed my plans without informing me, but it was hard to tell past the relief of not showing up late on the first day to train an army. Well, army might be generous. Squad?

"Do you plan on joining us?" I yelled as I pulled up my cargo pants. I so wanted to look the part.

"I have every intention of joining you," he replied from inches behind me.

I froze, relieved I had worn my cute underwear. "Does privacy mean nothing?"

"I've already seen everything. But I do enjoy seeing it again." He smiled as he leaned a shoulder against the frame. "The owls came last night."

"They did?"

"Yes. To the rooftop."

"Why didn't you wake me?"

"Because you were exhausted."

"Did they agree?"

"Yes. Of course they did. I've got good branches, remember?"

I moved past him and his all too charming smile into the living room where my coffee waited. As long as I had coffee, I could make it through. One day though... No, I wouldn't think like that. I had coffee today. That's all that mattered.

I looked down at the lists I'd made of the people who had signed up and were committed to this fight. "Squad" might have been overreaching a bit. It didn't matter, more people would sign up. They had to, because if they didn't...well, it wasn't going to be good for anyone.

"You ready?" he asked almost an hour later.

I looked up from where I'd been analyzing the list. I recognized most of the names on there. Out of everyone, it looked like the *changed* were the highest percentage of people staying. But the list was slim.

I looked at Cormac, gripping the sad list in my hand. He'd swapped out his normal business casual attire for something more akin to a bookie about to make his weekly rounds picking up the winnings. How did I know what a bookie wore on such outings? I'd prefer not to divulge. It was bad enough that I did.

"You don't like it?" he asked, indicating his sweat suit.

"It's just not what I'm used to seeing you in."

"I borrowed it from Dodd's closet. He's got a ton of them. He won't miss one when he gets back."

I made a slow silent "ahhh, now it fits," expression. I hoped he was right and that Dodd was coming back.

We left the penthouse and made our way toward the great hall. I was pumping myself up to make the best of the situation when I stepped in to face the beginnings of our army. It wasn't horrible, but it wasn't great.

Scanning the group, it looked like we had maintained all the Keepers. The ones that weren't stationed at the doors had shown up. We were down to a skeleton crew on guards, now that the wolves and Fae were defecting, so their full numbers weren't able to be here.

The *changed* made up the bulk of the crowd.

Redemption

All of the humans, Crash and his men, check...but where were Burrom and his Fae?

When I heard the sounds of laughter and a loud belch, I didn't make any outward reaction. On the inside, I was rolling my eyes and cursing. Framed by the stone archway, the most slovenly lot of Fae appeared with Burrom in the lead. Some stumbled, and there were random hiccups as they filled the space with the aroma of a brewery.

Burrom walked over to me and I was grateful he, at least, appeared to be sober.

"Are they all drunk?" Cormac hissed under his breath in Burrom's direction.

I didn't chime in verbally, just gave him my visual condemnation.

"Oh ay! Don't be throwing your judgments this way. You," he pointed at Cormac, "just left for months." He pointed at me next. "You never left, you were just drunk."

Both of us turned, shamed into silence.

"I thought so." Burrom crossed his arms across his chest as he stood next to us.

"Don't push it." Cormac said as he looked back to Burrom. "You'll go under again one day, and I'll find out where you're buried and plant a goddamn park bench right over your ass."

"You wouldn't!"

"With a colorful flower box full of daises right beside it."

233

"Thank you for coming," I said loudly to the crowd, cutting off any more arguments between Cormac and Burrom. "I know that what you have signed up for is frightening, but I will not ask for more than you can handle." I'm *so* going to hell for that whopper. "I'd like to start by everyone taking a piece of paper here," I held up a stack of sheets in my hand, "and writing down any skills you might have. Anything at all that might be useful. If you aren't sure if it's useful, write it down anyway."

They all quickly took paper and the pencils I offered and got to work listing their abilities. After everyone was leaning against a wall or a back filling out their sheet, I called Crash, who was milling around with some of his men, over to me.

Cormac and Burrom, who'd gone back to trying to one up each other, Cormac threatening tea roses now with Burrom countering with an orgy right in the hall, turned their attention back to me as he approached. They both took a step forward, now standing together as they eyed up Crash's approach. Well, I just found one thing they could work together on, I guess.

"What's up?" he said, the words were casual but they held a warmth that had me smiling back.

"I'd like you to head up firearms training."

"I'd be happy to."

"I didn't recognize most of the guys you brought with you. Do you have some men that can help?"

The conversation was feeling a bit awkward with the two nonspeaking participants hovering nearby but Crash didn't seem to mind.

"All my people are good with a firearm, but I've got some really great snipers in the bunch. As we figure out the skill levels and aptitudes, we'll pull out the ones with promise for some extra training." He turned to Burrom and Cormac, "You two good with that?"

They both made a couple of "hmphs," but grudgingly nodded.

Burrom walked away, Cormac didn't leave my side. Crash gracefully exited, rattling something off about needing to speak with someone.

Cormac stood behind my shoulder as I watched everyone finishing up their sheets. "I don't like him here."

"I don't believe he's the one that told the senator."

"But we don't know what part he played."

"You're right. But maybe sometimes people deserve a second chance." I knew I desperately wanted one in order to fix everything I'd help destroy.

"Does that go for everybody?"

"Everyone that promises to change their ways."

"So you're digging in, then?"

I glanced over my shoulder. "I thought that was

pretty clear."

"So, are you making this a challenge?" He leaned down as his hand rested on my hip. "'Cause you know how I react to a challenge."

Before I could think up an interesting retort, people were handing me back their sheets and Cormac was gone.

Chapter Twenty

Indestructible

We'd been training for days with no word from the owls and no idea of what exactly was coming. I'd finally managed to sneak out to clear my head.

I'd been avoiding Cormac since the other day. He hadn't been kidding about taking up the challenge. I swear every corner I turned, he was there waiting. I slept in the bed, I woke up with his body surrounding me. If I slept on the couch, I still woke up in the bed with him surrounding me.

If he couldn't break down my resolve with words, he was going to do it with actions and he had a lot to work with. I was starting to wonder myself what the point of holding out was, but then I remembered the three months of agony. I needed the promise.

I walked down the strip hoping no one had seen me slip out. Cormac would have had a fit with everything going on if he knew I was out here alone. But that was the point. I needed to be *alone*.

Then I saw him, the giant from right before the accident. He wasn't huge now, but the size of a common man. He stood, shimmering, a block away, there but not really. He didn't say anything, just stood looking at me for a moment before he turned and started to walk away.

I followed but not too closely, keeping my senses wide open for a trap.

"Come, I will not hurt you." It sounded as if it came from right next to me, but that was impossible. I couldn't tell if the voice was in my head or floating in the air for anyone to hear.

"How do I know?" I said, not loud enough that the man up ahead should've been able to hear.

"I will not hurt you."

It sounded like the truth but the voice was also not coming from a body so how reliable was it? "And I'm supposed to believe that because?"

I paused in the street, watching the figure get further away. Six months ago, I would have chased the phantom figure down, without thought to the consequences, but now I couldn't.

The senator loomed large in my mind. As much as I tried to prepare everyone and stack the cards in our favor, deep inside I was afraid that in the end, it would come down to the senator and me. I might be the last thing standing between a chance at a free life or mass enslavement. I didn't know who this creature was, but I couldn't succumb to curiosity, not if I wanted redemption.

I watched as the last glimpse of the man disappeared and felt the heaviness of regret fall upon me. I yearned for the days when my life was my own. With a deep sigh, I took my first steps back toward the castle.

***

I heard Cormac enter the room but didn't open my eyes. I was waiting for a sleep that refused to come and I wasn't ready to give up on it.

I heard him shedding his clothes before his weight shifted the bed, and he slipped under the covers with me. I didn't argue when he pulled me from the edge of the bed to the center, close to him. I told myself it was only because it was cold and he was warm, nothing else. I decided not to think any further on an excuse that might prove flimsy. His arm circled my waist, holding me tightly as one leg curled over mine.

"I've got to tell you something," he whispered in my ear.

A tickle of apprehension ran through me and I kissed the idea of a good sleep goodbye.

"Tell me," I said when he seemed to be hesitating.

He took a deep breath. His cheek resting so close by mine his exhale tingled my ear. "You thought I left you completely alone for three months."

"You didn't?"

"No. Not the way you think I did."

"Were you somewhere close?" My face was

scowling in confusion. He hadn't left? Why would he have pretended?

"No, I wasn't close but I would've known if you needed me."

"How?"

"Before I explain, I want you to realize, it doesn't really change anything."

He had both arms snuggly wrapped around me now and I was starting to think it had nothing to do with warmth and everything to do with self-preservation, his to be exact.

"What did you do?"

"We might be married."

"No we're not. You destroyed the contract. I saw it. I even kept it." I still didn't know what had compelled me to pick up that burnt carcass and then save it.

"I did destroy it. But things aren't quite as easy to terminate, anymore."

"Did you burn the contract or not?"

"I did." His arms got a hair tighter. "But it grew back."

"It grew back? I'm the one that has it. How would you even know that?"

"When I had your stuff brought up here when you moved in, I was trying to help you unpack when I found it on the bottom, underneath your things."

"You didn't unpack for me though." I never

unpacked that bag, no matter where I moved. It remained in the back of the closet. It was still untouched, even now, with things I couldn't bear to look at but couldn't part with either. The contract was buried underneath a bracelet Lacey had given me, a book of Monet prints and a birthday card from the Harveys, all remnants of the life I'd once had.

"I stopped after I saw that."

"What does that contract mean? What does being married to you in that way entail and how does that have anything to do with you not leaving?"

"It means I can sense when your life is in imminent danger. It doesn't act like a beacon or anything, but I'll know there is a problem. So while I was away, I knew you were okay. Up until that night I found you, anyway."

"Is that why you came back?"

"I would've been back anyway. The contract only allows a certain amount of separation."

"What does that mean? You would've been forced back here anyway?"

"Eventually."

"How long did you know?"

"Does that matter?"

"It's what matters more than anything. You kept this from me on purpose."

I tried to push at his arms to get some space but

he wouldn't budge. "Let. Me. Go."

"No. I'm not letting you run from me because you're afraid of commitment."

"That's not why I'm mad. You knew this and you didn't tell me? I sat here, devastated that I'd never see you again, and you weren't worried because you knew! Don't you think I was entitled to that information? Now, get off of me." I moved my head forward and then crashed the back of my head into his face. It startled him enough to let me break his hold.

I didn't answer as I walked into the closet to find that one bag. There, on the bottom just where I'd put it, was the contract, completely unharmed. I tucked it back in my bag for reasons I wasn't sure of myself.

"Where are you going?" he asked, holding his now bleeding nose.

"I'm leaving. But, unlike the explanation I got, you know I'll be back!"

"Where?"

In a mockingly familiar way, I uttered the same non-explanation he had given me the night I left. "I just need to go."

I yanked my favorite sweatshirt over my head and walked out.

**

I heard laughter within as I pounded on
Burrom's door minutes later. Burrom's floor was
now being called the den of inequity by most of the
castle.

"Hey! What's up?" he said as he greeted me.
This time at least he had pants on, if not a shirt.

I wasn't sure if I had smoke leaking out of my
ears but he instantly grew serious. "What's wrong?"

"Get rid of your chickies. I need to talk."

"Yeah, hang on."

He opened the door wider but I rested against
the wall outside his room while he cleared out. Five
women of various shapes and sizes, but all
attractive, left the room.

"All clear," he said, holding the door open even
wider and waving his hand in a grand gesture.

"Do you really need that many?" I said as I
walked past him and plopped onto his couch.

"I tried to downsize. Really did." He shut the
door and swaggered over to sit on the other couch.
"If anyone is to blame, it's you. You really packed a
punch when you sealed that ground." He reclined
back then eyed me up. "You're clearly out of sorts."

"Did you know?"

"Know?"

"The marriage, and don't play stupid." My
voice was deadly serious.

His mouth formed a silent "ooh" as his eyes
grew large. He'd known. Thinking back to some of

the comments he'd made in the past, I knew he would.

"I don't want to get in the middle of this shit."

"Why didn't you tell me?"

"It was only a suspicion based on my own contracts being stubbornly resistant to destruction, ever since the shattering. The timing of his return was also very coincidental, but I never knew for sure."

I didn't say anything, just sat there trying to sort it all out in my head.

"In his defense, he probably did destroy the contract. Things are really crazy, right now. You don't know what is going to happen when you dip into the magical stream these days."

"He should have told me." Months of not knowing if I'd ever see him again, wondering if he was dead, it all could've been avoided.

"Really, Jo? He was probably afraid of this."

"Do you think the contract is the only reason he came back?"

"Ahhh, now we come to the heart of the problem. And the old insecurities rear their head."

"It's a valid point."

"If the guy didn't have it so bad for you, it might be."

"Is my old room still available?"

"Don't be an idiot, Jo."

"He lied to me. Am I not allowed to take a

night to myself?"

"Your old room has been repurposed."

"Someone took it?"

"More along the lines of storage, but we had to move the furniture out to make enough room for our supplies."

When I raised an eyebrow, he threw his hands in the air. "It's not like we could put our stuff in the main hall. Take my bed. I've got a few others I can share."

"Thanks." I pushed to my feet before I fell asleep on his couch.

"And you might want to avail yourself of the clean sheets in the closet," he said right before he made his exit.

I made as little contact with the used sheets as possible while changing them out. Bed remade, all my fear of not being to fall asleep disappeared. I crashed as soon as I hit the bed.

I woke quickly a couple hours later when I felt strong arms lifting me from the bed in the darkness.

"It's me," Cormac said. "Go back to sleep."

"What are you doing?" I asked groggily but rested my head on his shoulder, too tired to fight.

"Bringing you back to our place. If you're mad, fine. I get that. I gave you an entire two hours away. Now you have to come back."

"You had three months," I said on a yawn, but I was too tired to argue anymore.

"Give it a rest, for now. You can fight with me tomorrow."

Chapter Twenty-One

Can't Fight the Numbers

It was the first real day of training. Cormac and I had been tiptoeing around each other since our fight a few days ago. Nothing was different, except the fact that I knew, but that seemed to be enough to put an awkward silence between us.

I understood his unease. He knew I was upset about him withholding something that important from me. He didn't get how much pain he might have saved me if there had been some guarantee of his return. I needed some time to work through the anger. So, for now, we were uneasy roommates.

I knew he felt guilty when he gave up the fake sleep act and relinquished the bedroom to me. I still found him on the couch every night.

This was going to be the most time we'd spent together in days. Crash had taken some of the humans to the roof for target practice. Burrom was teaching anyone that had a modicum of magic how to use it. That left Cormac and I to start on physical combat training. I was there for a couple of purposes. One, there were a lot of *changed* in our group of fifty that felt more at ease with me.

The other, and slightly more embarrassing, reason was that I could use a little fine-tuning myself. Unless I was channeling magic, I was abysmal at hand-to-hand combat when I came up against someone I couldn't zap.

We'd cleared the tables from breakfast service. Mats, rescued from the ruins of a nearby gym, covered the stone floor near where I stood, between Sharon and Katie. I'd been trying to rename Sharon "Ghost" for her ability to disappear, but I was having a hard time making the nickname stick.

Colleen edged up next to me, insisting on participating even with her cast, as we all waited for Cormac to start doing whatever it was that would turn our little group into a mean killing machine. I looked around at the bewildered stares and decided I'd settle for the equivalent of disgruntled holiday shoppers on Black Friday.

"So, Phantom, what's new with you?" I said as I looked at Sharon.

She nodded her head and didn't respond. I looked at Colleen and Katie, who both shook their heads as well.

"No good," Colleen said. "That's even worse than ghost."

"You guys have no taste."

They didn't have a chance to defend themselves as Cormac stepped into the middle of the room and cleared his throat, signaling he was ready to start.

"Thank you all for coming." He spun around slowly, making eye contact with the people that stood in a semi circle around him. "Today, we are going to learn some basic moves. I'll demonstrate first. Next, I want everyone to pair up and try the moves out on each other."

He was wearing a snug black t-shirt with athletic pants and he circled around, looking for his first training partner. Then he waggled his finger at me. I couldn't refuse to walk to the center, but I gave him a look as I did that made it clear I wasn't happy about his choice.

When he dropped to the ground, I knew I really wasn't going to like what came next. Lying on the ground, he looked up. "Straddle me."

Sometimes it was so hard to remain professional, but I needed everyone to take this training seriously, even if I was struggling. Who knew, it might save their lives, or someone else's, really soon.

"Now, try and strike me," he said loud enough for the whole room to hear.

I took a swing, knowing what was coming next but forced into a position where I'd have to just ride it out. I swung, knowing that I was doomed to miss.

He caught my arm in a grip that was impossible to move and I was on my back the next second.

"But she's not even half your size," someone called from the group.

"Thank you!" I chimed from the floor underneath Cormac. The group let out a chuckle and Cormac got to his feet, pulling me up with him.

"When the senator arrives, and we go to war, no one is going to match you up according to size. There is a good chance you will be outmatched and outweighed. There is no fair in war." He wiped his hands on his thighs. "I want everyone to spread out and find a partner. Take the same position we just did and try to unseat them."

I latched on to Colleen quickly, before he decided I should be partnered with him again.

"Yeah, I love you too," Colleen said as I clamped down on her arm.

I pulled her over to a clear spot on the mats. "Top or bottom?"

"Top? I guess?"

We were both fish out of water if we couldn't draw on a little magical juice, which we'd been forbidden to do for this exercise.

"What's going on with you two?" she asked as she got on top of me.

"We're in a bit of a funk."

"It didn't look like a funky place. When you guys were on the floor wrestling, it was pretty freaking hot. You guys must have mad sex."

"I don't want to talk about it."

"You aren't having sex?" her jaw was gaping and she was so shocked I used the opportunity to easily flip her over.

A shadow fell over both of us as Cormac came

to stand over.

"I need you a minute." He leaned down close to me so as not to be overheard. "The owls are on the roof."

I saw Buzz standing in the doorway, probably the one that had alerted him. I also knew the owls probably wouldn't speak to Buzz. Not only did they not know him, he wasn't *changed*.

"I'll be up as soon as I'm done," he said as I hopped quickly to my feet.

I walked out of the hall, not wanting to alarm anyone, and then ran as soon as no one was looking.

I was panting as I pushed the door to the rooftop open. The owls were perched on the branches of a recently planted tree.

"Where is the other one?" they asked. "The one with the good branches?"

"He couldn't come."

They looked at each other, obviously disgruntled at getting me, and I realized where the saying ruffled feathers came from.

"I like the other one better," one owl said to the other.

"I don't like this thing." The other owl twisted its head all sorts of ways before trying to grab the collar with its beak.

"Fine. Get these things off us."

They both lifted their necks where the collars with the cameras were.

"What did you see?" I asked as my hands fumbled with the buckles.

"Creatures."

I didn't bother to keep asking. The moment I released the collar off the second owl, they took off without another word, obviously not caring if they spoke to me again or not.

It didn't matter. All I cared about right now was what I'd find on the cameras.

Cormac was coming up the stairs as I was heading down.

"You left everyone?"

"Buzz took the lead and as soon as everyone got comfortable, I slipped out." He looked at the collars grasped in my hand. "You ready?"

"I'm hoping for a surprise." I turned and headed back toward the penthouse. So much had changed since I had first walked this hallway, now covered in stone. And if these cameras held what I feared, possibly so much more would be changing still.

Without a word, I started to pull out the memory cards as he went and powered up the laptop. Gone were the days when we would just leave them running. Power was the second most valuable commodity, just beneath food. As it was, there was only one computer we kept charged at all, for rare instances of need like this. It wasn't like you could look anything up on the web anymore. There was no web.

We stood shoulder to shoulder as we waited for the computer to boot up. I handed him the memory cards solemnly, as if I were handing a judge the jury verdict that I feared would read guilty on all counts.

Then the images appeared.

"What is that?" I said, running my hand over a group of buildings that all looked eerily similar.

"That's an encampment."

"It's big."

"Really big."

Flipping through the pictures you could see how close to the tornado wall it was located, also conveniently centered around a major highway that I knew lead right to us.

"We knew he had an army. This doesn't necessarily mean he's going to move on us."

"Look at that," he said, pointing to another picture with a line of trucks. "They're all inbound. There must be at least fifty of them driving in. Jo, there isn't a single one heading out."

"Maybe he just wants to be prepared for us moving on him?"

"When did you become an optimist?"

"I was trying something different out. Apparently I can't pull it off."

I don't know if he took my hand or I took his, but we stood there, hands grasped, as we stared at the pictures flashing on the screen.

"Cormac, you've been alive for centuries."

"Yes."

"Things like this happen from time to time. Right? Wars happen. The human race goes on."

"I wish I could tell you that this will be the same." His roughened palm tightened around my hand.

I'm not sure how long we stood there, watching the pictures of an army that dwarfed the amount of people we had.

"If they want to fight, they're going to have to come to us," I said.

"Agreed."

"We stock pile as much food and supplies as we can. And then we pick them off one by one as we stay safely tucked in here."

"With a little help from Jo, I could do some sick enchantments around this place," Burrom said. I'd been so transfixed on the images I hadn't even realized he was there. We both had been. I turned to where he was standing in the doorway.

Dark burst in carrying Harvey before I could get more details from Burrom.

"You need to take him," he said as he shoved a swaddled Harvey at me.

"Why are you covered in ash?" I asked having a horrible feeling it was linked.

"Dodd no longer has a couch because Harvey had the hiccups."

I looked down at his little face and he made a

small sound, like he knew Dark was mad at him.

"Ah, Dark, he didn't mean it. He looks so sad." I pulled him closer to me, rubbing his back.

"Let me know how you feel after you lose your couch."

"We've got bigger problems, Dark." Cormac pointed at the screen where the images were flashing.

Dark moved to the computer where Burrom joined him and they went back over the footage.

By time the night was done, we'd estimated the senator's forces at 10,000 against the measly 1,500 we had left.

Burrom left with the promise of meeting me in the morning to start doing some serious mojo to the castle. Colleen came and picked up Harvey for her turn, which left me and Cormac.

"This has been a bad day," I said, running a hand through my hair.

"I know you're upset about me not telling you about the marriage, but can we call a truce for now?" he asked, shifting closer. "I don't want to fight with you anymore."

I didn't fight when he pulled me to him and wrapped his arms around me. He held me in a hug, his hand rubbing my back.

"I should've told you. I know that."

I didn't relax but remained tense.

"Jo, for once in your life, just lean on me."

"How can I? The last time I did, you left." My words contradicted my actions as my hands started to move around him.

"I'm not going anywhere."

"I wish I could believe you." My arms dropped and then so did his.

Chapter Twenty-Two

Collateral Damage

It was fifteen minutes past nine. I raised my face to the sun and let it take the chill from my skin as I waited for Burrom.

The main throng of people looking to escape war had left, but people were still exiting in dribs and drabs. The fewer people we had, the more we had to scramble for any other possible advantages.

The wind kicked up a notch and I hoped there wasn't a storm heading in. I needed every truck we owned out gathering supplies, in case we'd have to hunker down as we picked the senator's forces off slowly from behind our walls.

"You're late. Do you think I have nothing better to do?" I asked when Burrom finally pushed through the front door.

He just smiled as he strolled over. "I get that you're new to this immortal stuff, but you need to stop sweating the minutes."

"If the senator wasn't gathering and army to march on us, maybe every minute wouldn't count." I looked around, "Where do we start? We need to get going. What's the plan?"

"I'm thinking that if we can seal the castle the same way we would for a resting ground, it would repel any who mean to do harm. That should cover anyone with the senator."

"Is there anything else?"

"That's the best I've got. The sealing is the strongest. Problem is, I've never sealed anything this big and even if I manage, I'm not sure how long it will last on this scale."

"Let's start. We've got nothing to lose."

"Actually, we're better off waiting until late tonight." He nodded toward the people walking here and there. "Unless you want to risk some crispy critters. We can't have anyone walking around when we do it."

"Then why are we meeting now?"

"Take a walk with me."

I followed his steps as he headed out of the courtyard. He didn't elaborate until we were halfway down the block but I didn't care, the silence was nice. Lately, all I did was talk to people. I'd gone from speaking so little to nonstop chattering. I didn't have enough of those kinds of words to go around.

"I wanted you to meet someone and I needed your morning to be clear."

"Who?"

"Someone that could help us, if they became so inclined. They've expressed a curiosity about you."

He tucked his hands in his pockets and I pulled my jacket closer as the winds whipped up.

"If we're going, let's step on it. I think a storm's coming and it's my turn to watch Harvey tonight."

"It'll be warmer where we're going," Burrom said, perhaps noticing how tightly I was curling my arms around my body.

"Nothing personal, but is it island warm or more along the lines of the fires of hell? You are walking a thin line these days. Who knows what new friends you've made of the underworld variety?"

The stories of drug induced orgies and other goings on danced in my head, literally danced, stripper pole and all.

"You know, maybe you should swing down, one day. It would do you a bit of good. You're getting very uptight, these days. You really need to get a little."

I pulled the hood up over my head to give me partial cover as I walked next to him. "Can people please stop concerning themselves with my sex life?"

He laughed before he spoke. "I'm not surprised I'm not the only one that's noticed."

"Where are we going?" I guessed we were about a mile from the casino by now and I felt like I was turning into a human popsicle. In another couple of minutes, I'd be welcoming the flames of hell.

He stopped and circled around. "Yeah, this

should do it."

"Huh?"

"Come here." He stood, arms out.

"Why?"

"Because we have to go underneath and too far down to do a big tunnel."

"What's down there?"

"The person that wants to meet you. He's a Ground Fae."

"Why can't he come up?"

"He's old school and doesn't feel comfortable topside. I swear, I don't know how Cormac deals with you. Can you ever just do something?"

"I want to be home by dinner." I stepped close to him and he wrapped an arm around me. I watched as the snow below us cleared completely until there was dirt, then the dirt under our feet sank lower and lower compared to the dirt at our sides.

"How long is this going to take?" I asked as we started to descend. I don't like heights, I don't like confined areas, and I was pretty sure I wasn't going to like deep dark depths, either.

"The longer he talks, the better. If we are out of there quickly, I wouldn't expect too much help."

I leaned my head against Burrom's chest and closed my eyes, trying to pretend he were Cormac. To Burrom's credit, he didn't mock my obvious distress once. I was certain I wouldn't have had the same willpower.

"Two more minutes."

Then he gave me a little pat on my shoulder as he heard me count to a hundred and twenty.

"We're here."

I took a step back until there was a few feet between us and I could pretend I'd had more dignity. As I looked down, I expected to see a packed dirt floor beneath my feet, not polished granite.

"Where are we?" My eyes started to adjust and I got a good look around. It was a cavernous hall as big as a theater. The walls also appeared to be a type of granite and the light from the many hanging candelabras bounced off the marbled surface, revealing the minerals and depth of the stone.

A single chair, which sat in the center of the far wall and was made of scrolling copper, appeared to be a throne of sorts.

Burrom urged me further in.

"What is this place?"

"It's the hall of the Earth King."

"And you thought it was a good idea to bring me here? I'm probably enemy number one. Have you seen some of my handy work? Did you somehow miss the tornados, the blizzards in Vegas? I could go on, you know."

He squeezed my hand and shook his head. "I explained it wasn't your fault. He knows all the details. He's my king." He shrugged like I should've figured that out.

Tiny fairies, no bigger than my hand, exactly the way I imagined they would look as a child before I'd met any, flew in carrying chairs.

Then a wizened old man appeared. He slowly walked across the distance, taking his time and not bothering to look at me until he sat upon his throne. Then his gaze locked onto mine. His golden eyes looked like they belonged to a much younger body.

He didn't speak but nodded his head at the chair near his. I didn't see an obvious exit as I hesitantly approached the seated man. He nodded again to the chair and I relented and sat.

His head angled to the side as his eyes took in every aspect of me.

"I apologize for our ill met earlier meetings. I really don't venture upward much and haven't projected in a long time. I don't always get the scale or placement right."

"You were the giant?"

He nodded.

"And on the strip?"

"Yes. My image tends to distort so I don't look exactly as I am. I used to have more practice, but haven't had the need in a long time. I've gotten rusty after all these years."

"What did you want to speak to me about?"

"You've caused a good deal of trouble."

His voice didn't sound like the old man he

appeared and I tried to focus on his shape. Was it a facade?

"I never meant for any of this."

He nodded. "If you had, you wouldn't be sitting here, right now." His gnarled hands ran along the fabric of his grey silken robe.

I didn't know if that was a threat or he simply meant I wouldn't have been invited for tea. Since he wasn't attacking me, I figured it would be best to not pursue it.

The only thing I was certain of right now was that I was out of my element. I had a strong feeling that no matter how old he appeared, he would be able to squash me like a gnat.

He leaned forward peering straight into my eyes. "What are your plans for the senator?"

"I'm not certain." Scary old weird man or not, he was crazy if he thought I was going to lay out my every thought for him. I shot a look over to where Burrom was standing in the back of the room.

"No, he has not divulged this information to me. I prefer to hear it from you, anyway."

"You'll understand my hesitance in sharing information with someone unknown to me."

"I'm aware of what is coming."

"Are you planning on taking part?"

"I haven't taken part in anything for a very long time, but I can't allow any more damage to occur."

"I'm not looking for trouble. This war is of the

senator's making." I leaned back against the velvet of the chair.

"I don't know if my Earth can handle anything more from the two of you."

"I'm not looking for trouble, but I won't sit idly by either as I'm attacked."

"And what of the additional damage you might cause?" He leaned forward in his throne.

"What would you have me do?"

"Surrender to him." He slammed his fit down onto the arm of his chair.

"And what of the people I protect?"

"I care not," he sneered. "Whatever lives they will have will be better than nothing."

"Are you asking the same of the senator? Why don't you ask him to give peace when he is the one so determined to have war?"

"I have. He will not bend."

"But you think I will?"

"No. I think I can make you."

"Then you are mistaken."

I turned to look to Burrom. I found him right behind me. My eyes shot daggers, silently accusing him of a set up, but he wasn't looking at me but at his king. He was angry as I was.

Burrom took another step, now side by side with me. "You said you only wanted to talk to her."

"I will do what's necessary." His voice rose louder with each word until it felt like the entire cavern was vibrating.

I turned to Burrom. "Are you with me or am I on my own?"

"I am with you."

"You would side with her? After everything she has done?"

"You are wrong."

"I'm leaving."

"I'm not done." The Earth King said.

"I am." As I rose to my feet and went to take a step, I felt the pull of his magic. He was trying to glue me to the spot and the pull was strong. My impression of his great strength might have been an underestimation him.

Instinct made me want to push against it but instead of fighting, I pulled the magical energy toward me. Absorbing everything he sent into myself, freeing my legs. I took a step toward Burrom, holding back the shaking but just barely.

"I'm ready to leave."

"So am I."

At the king's roared "No," I turned back to look at the king. The facade of the old man wavered over an image much closer to what I would have expected from the powerful being. A Fae, who didn't look a day over twenty-five, stood tall and proud in all his glory.

Waves after wave of his magic reached for me and I was absorbing it into myself. With each moment, his true form displayed a bit clearer, the glamour shredding from my eyes. I knew I owed the true vision to the amount of magic flowing into me.

"Now, Burrom."

"You got it, babe."

He held me as he started to tunnel us back to the surface. I could still feel his king's magic, reaching for me, as we made our way up.

"I didn't know."

I nodded. I was holding on by a hair and afraid to even speak.

"We're almost there. As soon as we reach the top, let it out."

I looked at him.

"I'm bringing you up somewhere uninhabited. I'll go immediately under again."

I nodded again and took a few breaths, afraid of even exhaling strongly. Magic was starting to seep from my very pores and I gripped Burrom harder, urging him to get there as fast as possible. I was thrust to the surface and I didn't even have a minute before I felt the power burst from me. I didn't check to see if he was underground, not having a second to spare. I thrust the magic from me with the energy of an atomic bomb splitting the atom. After it pushed out of me, I lay there on my back in the snow field, wondering how I was even in one piece.

I was exhausted and I might have lain there forever, if I hadn't heard a whistling sound on the wind. Now what?

I opened my eyes to the too vibrant sky above me and pushed into a sitting position as I saw gray blurs on the horizon appearing. I felt like I'd just fought twenty rounds in a no holds barred fight. I really hoped this wasn't more trouble heading my way, because I would lose for sure.

I spun around and saw Burrom rising from the ground amid the snowy fields.

"What is that?" he said as he noticed the gray blurs approaching quickly in the distance.

"I don't know."

He moved quickly, positioning his back to mine.

"I'm sorry about that. He told me he only wanted to meet you."

"No apology necessary." We didn't look at each other as we spoke, keeping our eyes on the newest threat.

"They're rippers," he said just as I was realizing the same.

"And new ones. They aren't solid."

Every part of myself tingled in true fear. It was me. Wherever they were from, was I the link? Did I bring them to this reality? Did I in essence, bare them into this existence? Was it I who brought them into our reality?

"Burrom?"

"Don't say it."

He couldn't have said anything worse. "So you think it's me, too."

"I didn't say that."

"Yes, basically you did."

They were coming closer and closer, their whistling noise becoming louder with their approach. They didn't stop until they were about five feet from me. As they stopped, I could see they were in different degrees of opaqueness. Only some of them must be new.

Slowly, they all started to bow their heads. I spun around, watching as hundreds, maybe thousands, of rippers slowly stopped.

"What are they doing?" Burrom asked.

I couldn't say the words. If I did, it would make it real.

When I saw Burrom spinning around frantically, I knew he was about to burst. "Fuck!" he yelled. "They're paying homage to you!" Then he turned to me. "Why are they doing this?"

Chapter Twenty-Three

The True Definition

"Why were they paying homage to you?"

"I told you, I don't know." Burrom must have asked me that question five times since we'd left the rippers out in the field. He'd tunneled us under the ground to the outskirts of the strip. It was a great enough distance from where we had been that it would be hard for them to follow. Not that they couldn't find me anyway, but I was going along with anything that kept Burrom calm.

"Why do you think they did?" Burrom continued to press.

"I don't know." The castle was in clear view with people milling around the courtyard. I wasn't willing to have a hypothetical debate here and now about how I might be bringing the rippers into existence here.

"Bullshit."

"I know as much as you do. And stop looking at me like I'm a Goddamn alien."

"Whatever you are, it isn't human."

"You're right. I'm half Fae, half Keeper." I walked toward the castle and prayed he'd drop the subject.

"There isn't a Fae in existence that can do the

stuff you just did. And Keepers are part human. You, are not human."

"Yes, I am."

"You're human the way a diamond was once a lump of coal."

"Stop it. This isn't the place." I signaled toward the bystanders trying to get some air.

"Is it what I think?"

"I really don't know."

Something seemed to click in him and he appeared to calm down a bit, as if he was moving from shock to acceptance. "I hope it's not what it looks like. Because, from where I'm standing, whatever is between you and the rippers is a hell of a lot stronger than I ever imagined."

I turned away from him again and continued to walk.

We reached the courtyard as Cormac stepped outside. Burrom nodded a greeting and took off.

I saw his eyes shoot from Burrom's back to me.

"What's wrong with him?"

"Not here," I said looking at all the people still around who could overhear.

I spent the entire walk up to the penthouse deciding on what to say. I thought of every lie under the sun. He'd know I was lying, but it still might be better than the truth. What if he looked at me the way Burrom just had?

I walked in the penthouse and I heard Cormac

lock the door behind us. For all the mental wrangling I had just done and the crushing fear of him looking at me the same way Burrom did, I decided, for once, I was done with the lying. The hiding. It was what it was. He'd left me before. I could get through it again.

So I told him every little detail and waited for the hammer to drop.

He didn't speak, just stared at the ground.

"That's what he was freaked out about?" he said when he finally looked up as if he didn't understand.

"Didn't you just hear what I said?"

"Every word. What did he think was going on?"

"Are you telling me you already thought I had something to do with the rippers?"

"I didn't know, but I'm not surprised after the other day when you called a horde of them." He leaned a hip against the arm of the sofa.

"Why didn't you say anything?"

"You didn't look like you were ready to talk about it."

I couldn't fault him there. I'd practically run from the crowd with hands over my ears, screaming "Nah, nah, nah."

"It doesn't bother you?" I stared hard now, looking for some sign of disgust or unease, but there was nothing. It baffled me.

"I'm not thrilled by it, but it doesn't change

anything between us. The way I feel about you doesn't come with a set of restrictions. There are no rules that say if you do this or you don't do that, I won't care anymore. This is just an aspect of who you are and I love you for the entirety of you, not for different pieces I can pull out."

I stood staring at this man, who accepted me fully, and it dawned on me for the very first time, he might be a better person than I was. I'd picked apart every action he'd ever made and weighed it by my scale of correct and incorrect, while he simply accepted me for everything I was.

I'd laid bare something to him that made Burrom squeamish. Something I myself didn't know if I would be able to handle, and he'd let it roll off his shoulders as easily as if I said it might look like rain today.

This was love. It wasn't what I had been expecting or had offered in return, but what he was giving me now.

I watched as he stood up straight and crossed the distance to me.

"What?" he asked as if trying to read my thoughts.

"I just didn't see it."

He reached out and caressed my face, waiting for me to continue.

"I don't think I ever really understood until this moment."

"You get it now?" he asked with a longing in his eyes that threatened to tear me apart.

I nodded. His hands reached down and gripped my ass, pulling me snug against him and I could feel his erection.

His lips covered mine, his tongue plunging into my mouth before he pulled back.

"Tell me," he said, both of us winded.

I pulled his mouth down to mine again as he pressed me against the wall. He pulled back, yanking my pants off and ripping them in his haste. I felt the swollen head of his penis barely breach my entrance then pull back.

"Tell me."

"Cormac, please." I squirmed closer to him but to no avail.

He pushed up my shirt and yanked down my bra, and then he took a nipple into his mouth. His fingers toyed with me but wouldn't give me what I truly wanted.

"Say the words."

"You know." I pulled at his hair in frustration.

"I want to hear it." The ridge of his penis ran back and forth, just barely entering.

"I love you."

He thrust forward and filled me completely, pinning my hips against the wall with his. It was as frenzied, as I knew it would be after so long. He pumped into me harder and harder and I gripped at him, wanting more.

My world exploded as I was gripped in an orgasm. He joined me with a final deep thrust. We both collapsed right there on the floor, and I laid my head on the crook of his shoulder.

Reality started to nip in again, all the more painful now that I had more to lose.

"What are we going to do?" I rubbed my hand over his chest.

"Right now," he rolled on top of me, thrusting into me at the same time, "more of this."

Chapter Twenty-Four

The Truth Doesn't Always Set You Free

"Jo..."

I bolted up in bed, a cold sweat on my skin, expecting to find the Earth King.

"Jo." It was the senator's voice.

I looked around the bedroom. I was alone. Cormac must have gone to do whatever it was he did while the rest of us who actually needed to sleep did just that.

I grabbed a pair of jeans and yanked a sweatshirt over my head. My hand pulled the door open slowly, peering out to see if someone was waiting in the living room. It was empty. I made my way out of the penthouse, and then the castle, without too many people taking notice. It was unfittingly sunny, almost cheery, in contrast to the company I sought out in front of the ruins he was partial to.

The senator was in front of the crumbled building, just as I'd expected to find him. He didn't turn toward me until I was nearly on top of him.

"I didn't think you'd come."

I didn't give him an explanation. What could I say? That I was grasping at straws, hoping somehow he had a change of heart?

"I've been told you know?" he asked.

I turned to stare at the ruins as well. I could still make out a couple pieces of roller coaster tracks.

"Yes. I'm aware of your plans."

"It doesn't need to come to this."

"I agree. I thought we had a truce."

"It didn't include him."

"I'm presuming you mean Cormac."

"I can smell him on you now." His facial expressions left no doubt of his feelings on the subject.

"What does he have to do with anything?"

"If you kill him, I'll stand my army down."

"Absolutely not."

"Then so be it." He didn't move though. "I loved your mother."

"I thought you hated her?"

"She was a pathetically flawed person, and yet I loved her. The wolves that botched your kidnapping, her killers, they would've died the moment they delivered you."

"Why are you telling me this now?"

He shrugged. "I would've told you long before, if you had asked. Your pride was the only thing in between you and knowledge."

"Then tell me now. I deserve to know. What happened all those years ago and what the hell am I?"

He took a few steps away from me and I stared

at his back, knowing the past would die with him; or, more likely, I'd die ignorant of it.

Then he stopped walking and turned back toward me.

"After I wouldn't do as the Keepers wanted, they imprisoned me in a different realm, as I told you. But Hammond, proud of what he'd created, would visit me. There was a portal, similar to what you would operate, that linked to the dimensional prison I was in. Sometimes he would show off to your mother, would entertain her by having me do tricks. He would allow me out, here and there, for her amusement, but they'd destroyed the shell of a body which had allowed me to remain in that world so I was weak.

"She wasn't a bright woman but, typical of a user, she recognized an opportunity. She knew that one of my initial uses was going to be to ferret out diseases in people, because I can invade them with little pieces of me. We realized that we both had needs the other could fulfill. She had been trying to get pregnant with Hammond's child, and I needed a body to host me.

"We struck a deal. She was unaware of the changes I'd planned to set into place. I'm not sure even she would have agreed to that. It took her a while to find a human that I felt fit my specifics. Not every human would be able to sustain my energy. As you know, she eventually found a match."

"What did you do to me?" I asked.

"Much more than I intended, that's for sure, or none of this would have come to pass.

"She came to me right after she had lain with Hammond. I sent some of my molecular energy into her and imagine my surprise when I realized she had already conceived without my help. She'd tried for nearly a year.

"You might have made it without my help, but that wasn't my plan. I knew even then what I'd need in order to survive in any real form. I needed a Keeper so strong that they'd be able to open up portals, even when no one else could. So I took some of the very material, the magic that helped create this new world, and I infused it into your very genetic matter.

"Then I just waited. I knew it would take a while for you to become strong enough to do what I needed. I also had to place you in the right spot. I had to parade you right beneath Cormac's nose.

"He almost screwed up my plans when he shot you. I thought his lust would overcome his ethics. I was going to kill him for that, and then he protected you in the alley. I knew then that it would work out."

I sat on a broken piece of cement, my legs weak. "So all along this was planned?"

"Most of it. I needed you to think you were

fighting against what I wanted, or you might have rethought some of your actions.

"Your father was just a waste. He figured out eventually but, coward that he was, he killed himself instead of telling you. He thought you would need his strength to close the portals. He didn't want to own up to his part in the destruction, so he handled it the coward's way and thought that would be the end of it."

"But I didn't."

"No, you didn't."

I rubbed my hands on my jeans, feeling numb. Bit by bit, the full picture fell into place.

"Lacey?"

"Yes. I was controlling her for quite a while. I needed to keep tabs on you. I needed to know when you were ready."

"Is she dead?" I'd always figured she'd died during the shattering. At least now I would know for sure.

"Lacey was dead the moment Cormac's man left her."

There was no anger in his voice, just a matter of fact retelling. It meant nothing to him, as it crippled me.

I wanted to curl into a ball but I didn't. I kept my face stalwart and an eye on his position. He would pay, even if it cost me my life. I would see him pay.

Even with the turmoil churning through me, I realized one very important point. "You can't control a Keeper. It would've been much easier to just control me directly. Or Cormac, but you can't."

He looked upward, toward the sky, as he shook his head. "I tried. Your bodies kill any part of me within seconds."

"So, how much of my life were you responsible for?"

"When your mother left you in the church, I lost track of you for a while, but I knew what to look for. It took some time, but I found you again when you were about ten. Then, when you were sixteen, you fell off the grid. That time was a lot harder, until you fell in with Oslo. I already had someone in his crew watching."

"And Oslo?"

"No. He was pretty crafty. I eventually had to put him down when I found out he was trying to organize a rebellion."

Put him down, as if Oslo had been a feral animal. I was having a hard time even looking at the senator anymore. My desire for more information warred with every instinct I had to lunge and attack him.

He casually walked along in front to the ruins as I watched him, and began to speak again. "The only thing I hadn't planned and didn't realize at the time was how intrinsically I was linking you to this new world. When I pulled its magic into you, to strengthen you, I didn't realize you would remain linked to it. I thought I could just take a piece of it. I didn't know it would stay connected."

"Now what? Even if you could, you're afraid to kill me. Why war? What is the point?"

He turned to me.

"Because if I can't get you to be with me willingly, I'll take everything you have left until you no longer care what happens. One by one, you'll watch them fall, and all because of you. Then you will either come with me or I'll take you when you no longer have anything left to fight for."

I've always wondered if anything was ever really all bad or if there was just a different ratio that tipped the scales in opposite directions. I used to believe that everybody had something redeeming about them. Staring into his cold chilling eyes, I knew I'd truly, and maybe for the first time in my life, stared down pure evil.

I couldn't let it happen. If war was coming, if he was set on doing this, I couldn't wait and risk more death.

I stood and opened myself up fully and pulled every ounce of magical energy I had to me with no real idea how I'd use it, just that I needed to end this now.

He knew instantly what I was about. He backed up a few steps and smiled.

"You didn't think it would be that simple, did you?"

Before I could draw any kind of significant power to me, he was gone in a tunnel of wind that blew dust and snow in my face.

I stood there. Alone, I let the tears of sorrow pour down my face. I cried for Lacey, Olso and the other countless deaths I couldn't even being to name.

And I cried to mourn the losses that were still to come.

Chapter Twenty-Five

And so it begins...

It was exactly one week since I'd seen the senator. Six and a half days since we'd started preparing full throttle ahead. And one day since the panic really set in, when reality hit and I knew we had almost no chance of winning.

I was sitting on the couch, exhausted. This was the first five minutes I'd had of down time today and I felt guilty taking it. I needed to get back up but I couldn't seem to raise my head from hands where it rested. Doomed. We were all doomed. This was how Cormac found me when he came in minutes later.

He walked over and stood before me, and I could see his shoes through the cracks in my fingers.

"I'm going to go out on a limb here, but I'll take this to mean you've given up on false optimism for the foreseeable future?"

"We need more." I grabbed handfuls of my hair and pulled at my scalp, wishing I could literally force the ideas from my brain.

"We've had everyone training until they drop. If we push any harder, they'll be burned out and useless. What more can they do?"

"That's the problem. I don't know and if we don't figure something out, we're dead." I burst to my feet with pent up energy. "That's not actually true. All of *you* are dead."

When he didn't argue, another needle of fear shot into me, adding to the collection. "No lies of how this will work out in the end?"

He walked over to the window and leaned against the sill, so calm compared to my own agitated state. "I can't tell you something I don't know."

"If it comes down to it, if it looks like we have no chance..." I didn't want to say the next words to him. How could I tell him I'd willingly walk away again?

"No."

"If it means-"

"No. Anything but that. Death would be better than an eternity with him."

"Death isn't an option."

I didn't bother continuing. I would do what I must, just as he would.

I watched his profile where he stood so I knew the very second something caught his attention. "What?"

"Do you hear that?"

I approached him by the window, angling my head. "No. I don't hear anything. What is it?"

"It's troops marching. A lot of them."

"He's here."

Cormac nodded and we both reached for our funny phones to set off the alarm and get everyone in position.

After alerting the entire castle that we would be under attack shortly, we raced to the rooftop. We'd just gotten to the edge with binoculars in hand when Dark, Colleen, and Burrom raced up behind us.

I held the binoculars and looked north. An entire army was marching our way. I went to hand them to Cormac but he passed them to Colleen.

"Don't you want to see?"

"I am." His trained his eyes on the far distance.

"No way. You can't possibly see that far," Colleen said.

"The senator is wearing a gold shirt under a gray fox fur."

I looked back to Dark, who was holding the binoculars now.

"Yep. He's right."

Dark handed the glasses over to Burrom.

"That's a lot of heat coming our way." Burrom dropped the glasses from his eyes and Colleen took them for another turn.

"How much time do you think?" I asked. "How quick does it look like they're moving?

Cormac squinted. "I'd say we've got until nightfall."

"Burrom, get every last Fae in the building and

meet me out front in a half hour."

"You want to try and do more shields? There's only so much we can do."

"And I don't think it's enough yet." I turned to Colleen, "The *changed*?"

"Ready."

"Dark, check in on Crash and make sure he and the other snipers are prepared. This is the plan. Remember, we stay inside as long as the wards work and pick them off from a position of safety. If we can dwindle their numbers, we'll have a chance."

"Dark," Cormac yelled, "Tell him there should be at least ten on the roof."

"Got it."

"How many do you think there are?"

"I'd say we're outnumbered nine or ten to one."

"Are you ready?" I asked.

"Yes. What about you?"

"Nope."

"That's my girl." He wrapped an arm around me and leaned down to kiss me. "Now, let's go kick some ass."

Chapter Twenty-Six

An Unlikely Alliance

I was standing at the bridge when I saw them come into view. A couple flew overhead, but the bulk of the senator's army approached on foot.

Cormac rested a hand on the small of my back. "Come inside."

"Why? I'm the only one they don't want to kill."

"But you are the one he wants. I don't want you anywhere in view of him." His hand circled and tugged at me slightly.

"No. I need to greet him when he gets here. If only to show him I'm not afraid."

"Fine. Then we'll do it together."

"I think you should go in. He wants you dead more than anyone."

"I'm not easy to kill, remember?"

He turned back to the rest of the people in the courtyard who were anxiously eyeing the approach.

"Inside." Most didn't hesitate longer than a few minutes before they scrambled in. I guess no one was too eager to die today.

There we stood, shoulder to shoulder, as we watched the senator approach, his army behind him.

"Cormac?"

"Yes?"

"I'm going to try something."

"Figured you might."

"Do you trust me?" I grabbed his hand and squeezed it.

"With my life."

"Once I let go of you, don't touch me for the next few minutes. I'm not sure what will happen if you do." I didn't know what would happen *period*.

"Don't overdo it."

"You said you trusted me."

"Yes, with my life, just not yours."

I laughed. "Don't worry. I'm not planning on dying today."

"Thanks. I'd appreciate that."

I stood on one side of the drawbridge, as the senator approached and stopped on the other, a wall of magical wards erected between us.

The senator's gaze took in my full measure before his eyes moved to Cormac, pausing where our hands held.

"You've made your choice?" he asked.

"There was never a choice."

I scanned the army standing about fifty feet behind him. Rulagh was in the front line, fury and hatred seething from him. Humans and so many *changed,* ready to do battle for him. But surprisingly, or perhaps not, there were no rippers.

Even though they had come seeking blood, my conscience couldn't help but feel they deserved a warning before I took further action.

"Leave here in peace," I yelled out to the crowd, "and I will bear you no responsibility in this. Otherwise, you will die here."

Nothing. No one stirred. At least I'd tried. The senator walked back to his people.

And I prepared to do what I'd been avoiding. The very thing that frightened me most, I was going to truly see what I was capable of. I just hoped I'd be able to live with myself after it was over.

"Cormac, step back away from me."

"I'm not leaving here."

"Fine, but make sure you're ready, because I'm not quite certain how this is going to work."

I took a deep breath, closed my eyes and concentrated. I could feel it tingle in my fingertips first as the power started to surge toward me. More, I needed a lot more, and I needed it quick before the senator knew what was happening and tried to stop it.

Our only hope right now was if I could level the playing field. This had to work.

It was rushing into me and I hated to admit how much I liked the feeling of the immense power I could feel at my disposal. I opened my eyes and I knew I was getting closer when I could see the magic swirling like colorful rainbow mists in the air.

I raised my hands and pulled it to me. The

heady feeling was seriously addictive. I felt the rustling of wind around me and realized I was building an eddy of power that must have appeared like a cyclone. So *that's* how the senator does it.

Unlike me, he didn't have this human form and all its vulnerabilities to contend with. As glorious as the magic felt, I could also sense it pushing my human weaknesses to the brink. And the senator was on to me. I needed to act.

I dared to pull a little more magic to me, and then in one large burst, I expelled it outward. The force of it leaving my system so quickly dropped me to my knees.

Then I waited and I didn't have to wait long. Rippers, more than I had ever imagined could exist, flooded the area. And somehow, without a word from me, they knew exactly what I wanted. They ripped into the crowd and the fighting ensued.

Blood spewed and shot into the air as they relentlessly attacked.

"Holy shit." I felt Cormac come to stand next to me.

We watched as blood spewed and I heard swords and daggers slicing through the air before they came down on the hard scaled skin of the rippers.

This was going to work. My eyes searched out the senator, who didn't seem to be able to get them under control. He'd known this was a possibility and it explained why he hadn't brought any rippers with his army. Even though I hadn't been sure, he knew I could trump any control he had on them.

Then the shooting started. The senator had been prepared for this possibility; a group of armed men and women that I hadn't noticed started spraying bullets down from their rooftop perches among the ruins. As they were still clustered around the crowd, it was easy to pick them off and still not harm too many of the senator's forces. And just like that, the rippers started falling to the ground.

"We knew it wasn't going to be easy," Cormac said as he heard my exhale. "Let's get inside. Our snipers won't open fire until you're further back."

"Why aren't the senator's snipers shooting at us?" I said. I didn't know if they could penetrate the wards but they didn't seem to be even trying. Then I answered my own question. "They don't want to kill me and they must figure it's not worth wasting the ammo on you. I wonder how they know it won't hurt you, now."

"I don't know, but I don't want to chance them giving you a try."

We retreated inside but not to hide. We'd set the castle up like an old town used to pirate attacks. If they broke through our wards, whoever was still alive would be forced to come in staggered. Cormac and the best fighters would pick them off one by one. But first they'd have to survive the snipers on the roof.

The wards were some pretty nasty stuff, though. I wasn't sure exactly everything they could do, but it would be painful, from what I could tell. They were layered so thick I wasn't sure anyone would be able to leave the castle if we lived.

I left Cormac to handle the first floor as my legs pumped me through the hallways then up the stairs. I pushed the door open and I saw all the snipers spewing bullets down upon the senator's men. Crash, gun in hand, was raining bullets down in between yelling orders.

"Get down!" he screamed right before a rain of enemy fire came at us. I was shoved to the ground.

I looked up to see Crash as he rolled off me. "Stay down!" he ordered before he was gone again. I crawled followed over on my hands and knees closer to the edge and where he was positioned again.

"Where's the enemy fire coming from?"

"That one." He pointed to the highest building near us. It had maintained its structure even if it was just a shell of what it had been.

"Can you get them?"

"We will. But until we do, they're making it real hard to do damage to the senator's troops."

When Crash and his people let loose another round of ammo at the senator's sharp shooters, I took the opportunity to appraise the situation below. The senator himself had already taken out part of the ward and steady streams of his forces were heading toward the castle entrances. I'd thought we'd have hours, maybe days.

I didn't fault Burrom and his spells. No one had ever come up against anything like the senator.

"Do the best you can." I patted Crash on the shoulder and crawled back over to the stairwell. I needed to get back downstairs. The situation was deteriorating so much quicker than I'd ever imagined and it didn't bode well.

When I hit the ground floor, the Fae were positioned along the windows, trying to reinforce the wards the best they could and block additional attacks. You couldn't gain access to the castle through the narrow windows, but you could shoot.

Cormac was handling the brunt of the intruders at the main entrance with ease. He didn't even look winded, but there was only one of him and there were a total of eight entrances.

I made my way to the side of the castle where Dark was covering another entrance. They'd already broken through the barricades there as well. There was nothing for me to do as he had it under control with Colleen taking care of anyone that slipped past him. There was a line of *changed* prepared to rotate in and out of the fighting. If I could help shore up the weaknesses, just maybe this could work.

I turned to leave and take stock of the other entrance points when I heard Colleen's cry. By time I turned around, the other *changed* were already pulling her out of the action.

I crouched down by her side as I saw the blood soaking through her shirt near her shoulder. A bullet hole from a lucky shot marked the spot.

"I'm okay," she yelled and tried to get up, in spite of me pushing her back down. Katie was on her other side doing the same.

"You're done fighting," I told her.

"It didn't hit anything vital." She sounded exactly like the pissed off teenager I often forgot she was.

"If you keep fighting, you'll bleed out."

"Katie, knock her out if you have to, but she's done."

As soon as she nodded, I got up and headed toward the other entrances. That's when it really hit me. Even if we managed to survive, as long as the senator was free, we would never have peace.

The senator was right. Colleen was alive but many others would die. How many was it going to take before I did what I knew I had to? Should I wait for a handful of deaths, or were thousands the amount I'd need before I stepped up to the plate?

I grabbed Sharon as she was running toward some of the windows with ammo. She and Katie were shooting the senator's people through the windows as soon as they got past the wards. "Where's Burrom?"

"He went to the second floor to try and get a better vantage point."

I nodded and ran off. When I found him, he was in front of a window on the second floor, his arms to his sides and his head tilted up.

"What?" he asked as I approached. I didn't even think he'd be aware of me there, his concentration seemed so deep.

"I need you to get me past all the people in the courtyard and near the senator."

His arms dropped and his gaze swung to me. "The floors here are stone." He shook his head and went to go back to what he'd been doing.

I pulled his arm down when he would've ignored me.

"I know you and, as such, you have an escape route. Don't bullshit me and tell me that you can't get out of this castle unseen."

"What if I can? Why would you do that?"

I felt a calmness come over me for the first time since I could remember. I knew what I had to do and I was at peace with it.

"This has to end."

"Why can't you wait and see what happens?"

"Because I'm the only one who can do it." I looked out the window to the senator, buffered by his troops about a hundred feet back.

"Get me there." I pointed to a small clearing near the senator.

"Are you sure you want to do this?"

"This has been my fate since the day I was conceived and I'm done running from it." I wasn't faking confidence this time. I didn't know if I'd live or die either, but I was ready to face what came. My whole life I'd been hiding and avoiding who I was and I was tired of it. Sometimes it's in your darkest moments that you learn to shine.

"Yes." Even as he was agreeing, he shook his head.

"You'll get me to him?" He so clearly didn't agree I felt like I needed another confirmation.

"I'll do it. Does Cormac know?"

"He'd use everything he had to stop me. If that didn't work, he'd insist on coming. I won't let him die for me."

Burrom nodded and silently led the way. With everyone's attention so fixed on outside, no one paid any attention to us as we made our way to the cellars.

"Do you have a specific spot in mind?" I asked as I followed him down the dark corridors, wondering exactly how he was going to funnel through stone.

He didn't reply, just kept walking until we reached the furthermost room in the hallway. It was used to store household items, like extra blankets and the like. I watched as he slid some boxes forward. He used his fingers to dig in the crevices around a particularly large stone. It was a fine sand, not the cement that should've been there. Digging out just enough until he could get his fingers on either side, he lifted the deep stone out of place, leaving a three feet by three feet area in its wake of dirt.

He stood up straight and wiped his hands off on his jeans. "It's going to be tight."

"How do you even fit in there?"

"Like I said, it's tight. Once I get past the opening, I'll open it up more."

He turned to me from where he knelt down next to the spot. "You sure you want to do this?"

"Yes." I clutched the flashlight I had grabbed on my way and tucked it into the side of my pants.

"I'll go first and then stop. You drop into the hole after me."

He funneled down into the ground and stopped, just as he'd said. I dropped into the hole after him, grabbed on to him for dear life and closed my eyes.

It was less than five minutes later when he stopped but I knew we were still underground, even before I opened my eyes.

"You're sure about this?"

"Yes. But, Burrom, if I don't make it, tell Cormac I loved him and I'm sorry."

"He'll understand." I felt Burrom's arms tighten

around me. "It's been real, kid."

"Same here. Now drop me off and get the hell out of here, okay?"

"Don't have to tell me twice."

I closed my eyes and, less than a minute later, I could feel the fresh air hitting my face, the smell of freshly churned dirt lessening.

I opened my eyes and saw the senator staring at me from ten feet away, the fighting still ensuing full force behind him. His people around him just stood still, as he did.

"This is unexpected, Josephine," he finally said.

"You were right. I don't want to watch them all die. I'm yours."

His face lit into a brilliant smile and he made a motion for his people to approach me, but I held up my hand and held them at bay.

"I have a condition."

His smile remained, but not quite as bright. "What?"

"I want you to send whatever it is of you that controls people into my body. I know you affect people's emotions. I want you to make it so I don't care about this place or any of them anymore."

His smile dropped completely. "You know I can't do that." The senator's hands fisted as he stood watching me. "This was a trick."

"No." I raised my palms up in placation. "I think you can if it's something I want. You've only tried on unwilling hosts. I want this. You do this, and then we will all leave here together and I'll never want to return to him."

"You want this?" He took a hesitant step toward me.

"Yes. I want to take you into me. It's the only way. You're so strong that I know you can do it." I held my arms out toward him, coaxing and hoping.

He took another step than paused. "I don't know."

"I can't hurt you. You created me. This is how it should be." I took a step closer to him.

He stood still for a minute and then with excruciating slowness, started toward me again.

"You're right. I can."

"Yes. You are the strongest being I've ever met." I waited patiently as he finished closing the distance. We'd gathered an audience, but everyone near the castle was still deep in battle. Please, let this work.

He was smiling again as he reached for my hands and I hoped that I was right, that this would work.

His hands solidly grasping mine, I saw his relief as his energy started to infuse me. I let him offer it willingly at first. I just prayed I was right, that I could maintain myself long enough to pull this off. God, he was strong. Less than thirty seconds and I could already see the magic floating in the air in rainbow swirls.

I could see him, his magic, but it wasn't attached to anything. When I stared down at my body, I could see the magic flowing into me. It was darker and isolated, unlike my own. His was a cancer, unwanted.

His eyes squinted. "I don't think it's working."

"It is. I can feel you."

"But, I can't feel you?" His eyebrows raised as confusion flashed across his face.

I tightened my grasp on him. I almost had enough, now. If I could simply hold on a little longer, I could do this. I watched as the strength of his magic started to waiver in front of my eyes.

"Stop." He pulled at me but I was much too strong now. I watched as I pulled his dark magic from him, and I could see the magic gain its brilliance again as it left him. This creature, whatever he was, never should have existed.

His form, needing the magic to exist, was diminishing as I drained him. He was losing tangibility, now almost just a sheer hologram of himself.

Please, I saw him mouth the words he lacked the ability to say. I trained my attention solely on him as a funnel of wind started to form around us. So close, I just needed to hold on a little longer.

Until I had absorbed everything he was. There was nothing left of him and I collapsed, nearly out of my mind. I shook with the need to unleash this power churning inside of me, but I couldn't even raise to my knees. I lay there, alone, in a funnel cloud of power.

"Give it to me."

I heard the voice come out of nowhere but I recognized the speaker. It was the Earth King.

"How?" I looked around my small empty area. I was alone.

"Place your palms on the ground. I will take it from you." I didn't question how or why, just followed my instincts and did what he asked.

Lying on the snow, cheek flush to the ground, I placed my palms face down. I immediately felt the pull of the Earth King upon them. I hoped my instinct was right, as I didn't know if I could stop the purge of magic that was happening. The magic I had taken from the senator was pouring through me into the ground. I watched as it seeped out, brilliant colors as it had never been when the senator possessed it.

The colors dimmed as the tornado wall around me started to ebb. When I had almost nothing left to give, I felt the pull of the earth subside and I lay there in the snow, amidst the senator's leaderless army. They were no longer fighting, lost for what to do.

"Jo!" Cormac screamed my name from across the courtyard and I watched him run to me.

I used the last of the energy I had left to force myself up. I got to my feet by sheer of will alone, and I wasn't sure how I managed to remain standing.

Cormac's arms were around me in the next second.

"He's gone." Tears ran down my cheeks for all to see and I didn't care. I clung to him. "I did it."

"Yes, you did."

I pulled back from him to assess the situation. I eyed the crowd, so subdued now. A *changed* covered in black scales was the first to move. He took a single step forward out of the crowd, knelt on one knee and laid his axe down in front of him, bowing his head. Slowly, the rest of the crowd followed until every last one had followed suit.

"If you leave now, I will not pursue you. If you don't…" I let my words trail off, the threat clear.

Cormac's hand still in mine, we walked back through the crowd toward the castle as they retreated from it.

Everyone parted as we walked and Cormac's arm circled my waist. "Only a little farther."

I nodded but didn't speak. I was barely holding on; defeating the senator had taken everything I had and more. I saw the crowd part in front of us as my vision blurred, black spots starting to blur together.

When I felt the bed underneath me, I didn't recall most of the walk there. Cormac's body curved protectively around me. I tried to fight the draw of sleep but couldn't seem to keep my eyes open.

"Who's…"

"Sleep. I'll take care of everything." His hand ran through my hair as I rested a cheek against him. "I'll be here when you wake."

I nodded, succumbing to the pull as I heard his last words.

"I'll always be here for you."

Chapter Twenty-Seven

Paid in Full

"You sure you're ready?" Cormac asked me as we made our way to the ground floor.

He'd been hovering over me since the senator's death last week. I understood his concern initially; I'd barely been coherent the first few days, only waking to eat. But I way past the point of cabin fever.

"Cormac, I'm fine. I want air."

He smiled and there was the same twinkle in his eye I'd seen that last few days. It was that made me wonder what was going on.

"Are you going to tell me what it is that you are so happy about?"

He tugged my arm and drew me close. "You'll see."

"No word from Dodd yet?"

"No, but I'm sure he'll eventually turn up. Especially now that the senator killed so many of the rippers, it's a lot safer out there."

I remembered the senator's snipers spraying into the group of them until they were all but extinct. As long as I didn't do a mass release of magic into the world again, their numbers shouldn't cause a significant problem.

He pushed open the door that led us outside and I braced myself for the cold that didn't come. The snow was gone, leaving the sodden earth beneath.

"It feels like spring." I ripped off the heavy down jacket I was wearing and lifted my arms out to soak up as much of the sun as I could. The courtyard was filled with people sitting outside and children running and playing. It didn't just feel like spring, but looked and sounded like it. Laughter and children giggling rang through the air, sounding more beautiful than any music I'd ever heard. The smell of wet fertile soil and grass met my senses.

"How long has it been like this?"

"It's been getting warmer every day." He held out his hand to me. "There's more."

"More?" He smiled and nodded. I took his hand as we walked out of the courtyard as kids dashed in front of us playing tag.

We crossed over the drawbridge and I wanted to cry when I stepped into the middle of the Vegas strip. Every place that had a crack of dirt, which there were many, had flowers growing up through it. Flowers that weren't even native to Vegas sprouted as if they had every right to be there, tulips in every color, crocus and daffodils.

"How can this be?" I asked.

"I don't know," Cormac said.

Then, out of nowhere, a shimmering image of the Earth King appeared in the middle of the road. It wasn't the grizzled old man but a powerful male in his prime. *Because of your actions, I can now heal the earth. Your debt has been paid.*

He smiled and bowed to me, then he was gone.

"What are you looking at?"

"You didn't see him?" I turned and stared at Cormac who looked bewildered.

"Are you okay?"

I felt the tears on my cheeks he saw falling. "I'm perfect."

Visit us on the web at DonnaAugustine.com